Silence in the Silos

Michael Ramos

Dedication

About the Author

Contents

Prologue

The summers of our childhood were the best times of our lives. Riding our stingray bikes, running through sprinklers on the hottest days, and family picnics in the Santa Ana River. Eating *push-up* ice creams and loving a new pack of bubble gum baseball cards. We made our own baseball fields, and in-between innings, we ate pomegranates off my grandma's tree. Tops and Yoyos were all the rage, and if you mastered the *walking the dog* trick, you were cool, and you were to be home by sunset. The evenings were filled with family and friends sitting on the front porch. Yes, we had porches in those days. But nothing can beat listening to 45 records with my cousin, Frank. It truly felt like a *magic carpet ride*. There were no cell phones or social media, and the best television shows were Batman, The Flying Nun, and the scary series The Twilight Zone, as well as Outer Limits.

Those were the greatest days of my life.

PART 1
The Beginning

Chapter 1

It was the end of the school year, the Sixth Grade in 1970, The Beatles, Abbey Road Album was on my records player, and Roman Gabrial was slinging footballs for the L.A. Rams. Hot California Fridays were the best day of the week for this hyper boy, and the PTA moms selling ice cream popsicles after school made it even better. On Fridays, I would save my lunch money to purchase not one but two popsicles to eat on the way home. Well, one of my homes—Grandparents Hernandez's home. They lived two miles from Victoria Elementary School. It was a rural area and a great place to grow up. The town was nicknamed Okieville, as families moved here from Oklahoma during the Great Depression and Dust Bowl. Needless to say, we were lower-income households with middle-class values.

The walk home was on a dirt path through fields, and there were two huge grain silos that stood out like two giant cement stacks facing the sky above. On hot Fridays, the popsicles would be a treat walking home. However, one given Friday, to my surprise, my dad was waiting for my brother and me after school to drive us home to our other grandmother, Grandma Garcia's home. My brother was a year younger than me, and we lived in Colton, California. My dad took us to school every day and picked us up from Grandma Hernandez's home after he got off of work. My dad worked at Norton Air Force Base and had been single for twelve years after my mother committed suicide— more about that later.

Well, so much for my walk home to enjoy my just-purchased popsicles. Fearing my father would not be happy that I spent some saved lunch money on these ice-cold treats, I stuffed one in each pocket of my jeans for the eight-mile-or-so ride to Grandma Garcia's house. After the ride, I raced to the shed *Quardito* in the back of the house and pulled both melted treats out of my front pockets. Of course, when I walked back into the house, my pants were soaked, and Grandma Garcia asked me in Spanish, "Que Paso?" What happened? Embarrassed, I told her the story, and she smiled, telling me you should have told your father and shared one with your brother. Lesson learned, don't hide the obvious, especially if they melt!

Not easily done, as my father was an ex-U.S. Marine, and he believed in discipline and following rules at all times. In fact, as I look back, I was afraid of him but, at the same time, respected and loved him. His strength and discipline laid the foundation for the rest of my life and that I will always be grateful for.

As I look back, they were the best days of my life.

Chapter 2

Life felt like a ping pong ball through elementary school, bouncing from one grandmother's house to another. However, my brother and I felt loved by this huge, wonderful family that took us in at a very young age. Imagine raising a toddler and a one-year-old baby as grandparents well into their 60s. As I think about that, I can't imagine how they endured the energy of two young boys, but they did and did it well. My pop, on the other hand, was an *in-and-out* dad as he lived with his longtime girlfriend in another city while we stayed with our grandparents. I guess you could call him a *weekend* dad in the early years—but he never abandoned us. I was always proud as I was Anthony Garcia, Jr., and my father was Anthony Garcia, Sr.

That summer of '70 was one of the hottest in California. I recall having the upper bunk on the bunk beds my brother and I shared, and it was even hotter in bed in the small room we shared with my uncle. Thankfully, my grandmother always had a crate of oranges she would purchase from local migrant farm workers. Not only were they delicious, but they were cool and refreshing during the heat waves. We also survived the heat by making our own coffee can sprinklers, punching nails in the bottom of the can, attaching the water hose *(mangeta),* and hanging it from the only tree we had in the front yard. That, along with a water cooler, kept us cool during the day. T-shirts and ripped jean shorts were our summer attire.

My grandmother lived near the railroad tracks, and it was really cool listening to the Santa Fe trains rumble by the small house, but it also brought *trampas,* homeless men riding the trains to get from Southern California to the Central Valley to find work in the fields of various agriculture farms. At least once a week, a man riding the train would knock on my grandma's back door, seeking work or something to eat. You see, the word spread quickly that my grandma's house was a friendly place to get a meal. Whatever she had on the stove, she would make a burrito for them and then would send them on their journey. I recall being scared of these mostly very thin, unshaven men in tattered, dirty clothes. However, as the years went by, I realized that they were harmless and always very grateful for my grandmother's kindness. It's a lesson I keep to this day; some call it the *Golden Rule.*

We didn't have much money back in those days, but we never went hungry. Every morning I could hear my grandma pounding the *masa* as she prepared her amazing flour tortillas. I could hear the roller turning the fresh balls into a perfectly round tortilla, and the smell of fresh flour on the stove was like walking into a bakery. When she finished her first job of the day, she would then sit down and treat herself to a fresh cup of coffee with a piece of pan dulce. This would get her ready for the rest of the day. As for me, I couldn't wait to get up and spread some butter on her freshly made tortillas. It was heavenly good.

As I grew older, I would spend most of the summer with my maternal grandparents as they owned a much bigger property located near all my cousins and schoolmates. As well as it was in the rural part of our county, and I loved to be outdoors. It was like being at a family camp!

Chapter 3

Her name was Christine, but everyone called her Chris. Her mother was the PTA president I purchased the ice cream from. She was what we called, at the time, a *tomboy.* She was as fast as any of us boys, and I would always pick her to be on my team, whether it was Four Square or Touch Football. Yes, football, I daydreamed that I was the Rams Quarterback, *Roman Gabriel,* at that time, and she was my wide receiver, *Jack Snow,* another Ram player at the time. She was so fast that she would blow by the other sixth graders and had the softest hands ever. She could catch a football with her eyes closed. Needless to say, we never lost a game that year during our lunchtime games. She was also the smartest kid in school, and every boy in class had either a crush on her or was jealous of her popularity. As for me, she was my best friend and more like a sister to me.

One day, while walking home from school, I remember Chris laughing at me as my *Batman* lunch pail fell open and all the valentine cards I had been working on for days dropped out. "Are all those for me?" She asked before grabbing a handful and taking off running. As I said, she was fast, so instead of running after her, I picked up a rock and heaved it toward her. Just my luck—or not my luck—it hit her behind the head. She stopped, turned around and looked at me, and then kept on running home. After I got to my grandmother's house, there was a knock on the door, and there stood Chris with her mother. She held the rock in her hand that I had thrown at her. My grandma was not happy, nor was Chris' mother. She had also called the principal at our school, and I knew then I was in deep trouble. Lucky for me, my grandmother did not tell my father, but I was put on restriction for a week! The next day at school, I was called into the principal's office. I was afraid I was in deep trouble. My punishment was to take a wheelbarrow and go out onto the school's dirt field and fill it up with rocks. Needless to say, I never threw another rock at anyone. As I look back, it was a good lesson learned, and I was also to apologize to Chris. After she laughed about all the rocks in the wheelbarrow, she forgave me.

Chris was a tough girl. Her family had moved to the area from Oklahoma during the 1930s when dust storms greatly damaged farmland. Hundreds of families moved west to California to seek a better life for their children. Her grandparents moved here, along with her 10-year-old mother and her siblings. The approximately two square mile community was where many families settled down to establish a home and start a new life; thus, the name *Okieville*. It's not an endearing name, but everyone seemed to accept it as it had no negative connotation.

Chris' mother, Mrs. Stone, had her in 1957 and her two brothers, twins, in 1960, Johnny and Bobby. Mrs. Stone had a job at Norton Air Force Base as a clerk and worked there until the day she left. Like me, Chris was raised by a single parent as her father left the family after the Dust Bowl to move back to Oklahoma. It wasn't as if the family had a say in the matter, as he left in the middle of the night while they were all asleep in their three-bedroom house two blocks from school. You see, Mr. Stone had an alcohol problem, and he could never keep a job longer than a few months, but he sure could find a bar stool at the local bar where he would spend most of what little money he made. It was on more than one occasion when Chris was just seven years old that she would go looking for her dad at the local drinking hole whenever there was an emergency at home or the day a small earthquake hit. Yes, it happens in California, and she and her brothers were scared out of their minds. As always, Mr. Stone would tell Chris to go home, and he would be there shortly. Sometimes that was an hour; other times, it was in the early morning hours after everyone was asleep.

One afternoon in the Fourth Grade, I believe, I followed Chris home from school as she wanted to show me where she lived and her model collection that she was very proud of. Back then, we were all building models of supercars, like the *Snake G.T.O.* and the *Batmobile.* The best was *The Munsters'* mobile. Chris, on the other hand, glued the Monster Collection together—Dracula, the Mummy, Frankenstein, etc. It was weird but kind of cool at the same time. As we got to her house, I could hear loud banging and someone arguing inside. Chris looked at me and apologized, telling me her dad must be drunk again. It was three in the afternoon. Mr. Stone was yelling at Chris' brothers for not doing their chores, and they both ran out of the house after they were kicked by him while in his rage. I asked Chris if she would be okay, and she said yes, as she and her brothers would hide in the silos down the street until her mother got home. As I look back, I now know where Chris got her toughness from. From that day forward, we became good friends and got along well… except for the rock incident, of course. To this day, I think about why kids grow up to be not so good while others are successful in life, and as they say, it all starts at home.

In the summer of 1967, The Beatles released "All You Need Is Love," and my personal favorite at the time was "I'm A Believer" by The Monkees. During the summer, I would stay all three months at my grandparents' house in Okieville. They, along with several of my aunts and uncles, had homes on six lots next to my grandparent's house. We lived around the corner from the Santa Ana River, and we would spend days in the river water, packing a lunch and not coming home until the sun was down. It was some of the best years of my life. In the evenings, Cousin

Frank and I would play 45 records till late at night, and as The Turtles sang that year, we were "So Happy Together."

It was this summer that Mr. Stone decided to *hit the road Jack,* and all I heard Chris and her brothers sing was... *and don't you come back no more!* She tried to act like it didn't bother her at all, but beneath her armor, I knew she was hurt, so I did my best to be her friend. Chris' mother worked all summer, and she and her brothers stayed with her grandparents during the day. Every other day, Chris was allowed to hang out with us down at the rivers. Of course, she was the best swimmer and fearless, jumping off the rocks into the water. There were some very hot days, but we had huge trees to camp out under with ice-cold lemonade made from fresh lemons off my grandmother's lemon tree and *Wonder Bread* bologna sandwiches.

Life was good as we frolicked in our cut-off jeans and t-shirts. The evenings were just as fun, playing cards with my grandparents and aunts and a fun game of Yahtzee with my aunt from Los Angeles. In the mornings, after breakfast, I would go outdoors and call my cousins from the fence between the yards. We would start the day picking walnuts off the walnut trees and plan the day. There was never a dull moment, and, of course, there was no such thing as video games. Everything we did was outdoors, and boy, was it fun. As summer came to an end, as always, it brought along a mixed feeling of sadness and excitement about getting back to school to see friends and a new teacher. It also meant the daily grind of living between two homes, but it was how we lived, and I actually missed my paternal grandmother.

Chapter 4

It was 1970, the last day of elementary school. My dad had been gone for about two years now. We missed him, but it was much better at home. I was also lucky to have a best friend in Anthony Garcia, a kid just like me in many ways—funny, an athlete, and from a huge and fun family. Plus, he shared his twinkies with me! But things weren't always like that between us. When we first met—I believe it was the fourth grade—he would make fun of me because of my *frizzy* hair. I was born with hair like that, and it made me who I am, HA! He would call me Bozo the Clown, a famous television character at the time. I tried to ignore him, but it was so annoying that I finally challenged him to a foot race as he thought he was so cool and the fastest and smartest kid in school. I told him the winner would get a pack of *Flower Power* stickers and Bazooka bubble gum—it was on!

We lined up at lunchtime to run about one hundred yards on the grass playground, where we later played some great football games. Most of our classmates were out there cheering one of us on. I had no fear, as I truly believe I was born to be wild. Yes, thank you, *Steppenwolf,* for writing a song about me. We lined up, and Anthony said, "Let's go, Bozo," and I said, "Let's see who the clown will be after." Johnny was the starter, and he gave the good old *on your mark, get set, go!* and off we went. I had my P.F. Fliers on and felt like a supergirl as we took off. Halfway, Anthony started pulling away, but I would not give up. When he was about twenty yards from the finish line, he turned around to laugh, lost his step, and fell flat on his back, at which time I flew by him like a rocket. Everyone cheered, and I said, "Who's the clown now?!" From that day forward, Anthony never teased me about my hair again. In fact, he picked me first on his tag football team for the remainder of elementary school. Anthony called me *Jack Snow* after some Los Angeles Rams player. I will say that we never lost a game.

After the race, I told Anthony he really won, and I had his stickers and bubble gum at home. I asked if he wanted to come by after school, and he said sure. I was hoping my dad wasn't home, but that would not be in the cards. My brothers had beat me home, and as we approached my house, I could hear my dad yelling as my brothers ran out the front door. They said Dad had hit them, and he was angry about the house being a mess. I turned to Anthony and said I needed to go with my brothers to our hiding place, the silos. Anthony ran with us. Luckily, this time of year, the silos were empty of the wheat they would hold for the farmers. We sat there and played a game of *Trivia* until my mom came home from work. I was embarrassed that Anthony witnessed such a scene, but he never mentioned it again.

As I look back on these days, I know it's where I got my toughness and survival instincts.

One night when we were all asleep, my alcoholic dad decided to abandon us and went back to Oklahoma. We knew that as my mom's sister called and told her she ran into him in a bar, of course. My mom and brothers were upset, but, as for me, I was relieved and felt like it was a new world.

The summers in Okieville were filled with fun—having our own river, the Santa Ana, a rock's throw away. Speaking of rocks, I did forgive Anthony for his perfectly thrown pass to the back of my head. The river was a constant flow of happiness with friends and family.

Chapter 5

It was always a fun day, but today was really special as it was the end of Sixth Grade, and next year, we would be off to Junior High School, or Middle School as they call it now. The best part of the day was the Teachers vs. the Students Softball Game at the end of the day. My Sixth Grade teacher was retired Marine Corps and loved sports. He took the game seriously and was the pitcher for the teachers' team. I was the captain and pitched for the students. It was a slow-pitch game, but the pitcher had to cover a lot of ground. Of course, my shortstop was Chris. Not only was she fast, but she had a cannon for an arm.

Before we get to the game, here is a little bit about my competitive Sixth Grade teacher, Mr. Anderson. Every Friday, he would challenge his students to a game of checkers in front of the whole class. Of course, he was undefeated. However, if you could ever beat him, he would give you a jar of rock candy. He taught us how to make candy in our science lessons. Well, it was my turn at the end of the day on Friday. The other students were to read their *weekly readers* magazine while we played, or they could watch the match. My dad always taught me to play defense and make my moves to block my opponents, win or lose. Well, I was on fire that day, and after close to thirty minutes, Mr.

Anderson was frustrated and called it a draw. We both had no moves left. He was not very happy, but my classmates were cheering! I will say this, he did give me a stick of rock candy for the tie, and it tasted so good. I don't think I have had rock candy since.

Back to the game...

It was so much fun playing and laughing with my Sixth Grade classmates before we all moved on to Junior High School. Some I would miss more than others, but I will never forget my best friend, Christine. I say that because she disappeared, literally. Her family moved away, and I was never to see her again, or so I thought. That is when the nightmare began.

Chapter 6

Fast forward to the year 2003. I had been a Deputy DA in the District Attorney's Office for thirteen years. I was part of the Major Crimes Unit and had 125 jury trials under my belt. As I look back, my passion for victims started the day my mother committed suicide at the young age of 24. I had this drive inside of me to amend what happened. Throughout my school years, I wasn't sure how I was going to accomplish this until I decided to go to law school.

My cases in the last few years had all been murder cases. Each case presented a different challenge with regard to the evidence and the challenges in the courtroom. I had just completed a murder case when I heard the news from my sheriff investigating partner, Dean Liter. During the excavation of the fields where the two silos were located in Okieville, some human bones were found. A forensic anthropologist was now in the process of determining whether they were human or animal bones, but I kept on having the same thought, Christine. I had to sit down as it took my breath away. I'm not a fan of tilt-up buildings, but at times there is a positive to losing our rural roots to modernization. This may be one of those moments. I immediately asked my boss if I could handle this case. I was given the assignment, and if the term *'cold case'* ever described an old murder, this was it. I knew if it turned out to be who I thought it was, it happened over thirty years ago.

I met with Detective Dean Liter at the Coroner's Office to meet with the Forensic Anthropologist. As I looked at the bones laid across the metal table, I couldn't help to think of my best friend Chris and what, my God, had happened. We were fortunate that all or most of the bones were discovered, including the skull and the jawline, which included teeth.

The results were not surprising. The bones were of a human between the age of 10 and 15 years. What little clothing was left gave us some clues as to how she was killed. There was a jagged rip in the blouse she had on. It looked like a knife or sharp object wound as there was a hole in the front and back of the blouse, an entry and exit wound perhaps? There was no sign of a bullet wound, at least in the bones that were found, and we couldn't prove strangulation as the hyoid neck bones were intact, but that doesn't mean she could not have been strangled. Usually, you would find bruises on the victim's neck and petechial hemorrhage in the lining of the eyes, a sign of terminal asphyxia. However, none of that could be found at this stage of her death. As we left the coroner's office, I couldn't help but think of the past, and the emotions took my breath away. Detective Liter asked if I was okay. I told him, "No, but we will solve this case, and justice will be served!" First, we had to show these were actually Christine Stone's bones, a task I was not looking forward to.

We proceeded to take the next evidentiary step. Taking the jaw and teeth and getting them to a forensic dental expert. Dr. Hall was just the man for the job. He had helped me solve many murders by looking at the remaining teeth and comparing them to the dental history we prayed we had one. You can also get DNA, but we needed some DNA from the family. The new familial DNA could be a significant help in identifying the victim. A trip to Oklahoma was in our near future.

As I got back to my office, I couldn't help to think about the last time I saw Chris and how sad I was the day I heard her family moved when she went missing. I always thought that she just ran away and was having a good life with her own family in this world.

As I sat there, I got a call from Detective Liter.

"Tony," that's what Liter called me, "we found a small piece of possible evidence in her jeans pocket, a small folded-up flower power sticker. Any idea what that means? Do you recall her having such items?"

My heart sank. But I needed to go into fighting mode. This case was going to be very difficult to put together. Even if we identify the body, how and who would kill Chris? It was truly a *cold case,* but it's never cold to a family or for me, for that matter!

Our first step was to figure out who saw Chris last and what and where are the Stone Family. We began by looking up the family. We found that the father, Mike Stone, had passed away ten years ago. You guessed it, due to liver disease. However, the remaining family members were in Oklahoma. Now it was time to let the investigators do what they do best, put the forensic puzzle together. I was fortunate to have the best homicide detective in Dean Liter. He had a distinguished career in the Sheriff's Department before landing in the homicide unit. Yes, he had several officer-involved shootings, but they were all justified because the bad guys got what was coming.

Chapter 7

The summer between Fifth Grade and Sixth Grade was one of the best ever. The first two weeks started at Grandma Garcia's house in Colton. My brother, Arthur, we all called him Artie, loved sleeping in and eating handmade fresh tortillas for breakfast with eggs and refried beans. Then we would head outside to spend the entire day playing with our South Colton friends or our cousins that would come to visit. It was all about Hot Wheels and plastic army men while digging trenches in my grandma's gardens around the house to create our own little towns for our army and cowboys and Indians. However, the best was the making of our own water sprinkler systems to cool us off in the heat of the summer. You know, a coffee can with nail holes and running the water hose through it and hanging it from the tree. It was a great way to stay cool as we spent hours running under our outdoor shower. Of course, we would have a *water wiggle* or *slip & slide,* but we couldn't afford that. Oh well, we had fun. It was that summer that my dad surprised us with our *stingray* bikes. We were so excited, mine was lime green, and Artie's was metal-flake orange. Both with banana seats and sissy bars. It was like we could go anywhere now. Since it wasn't as remote as Grandma Hernandez's house in Okieville, we were only able to bike to the small Mexican Market and back, but we managed.

As for the store I mentioned, it was across the street from the Catholic Church we attended and where my father was an Alter boy through high school. The priest, Father Valencia, was good friends with my grandma, and he was like a second father to my dad. However, going to church was a drag for me on Sunday mornings. Why? Because the *Adventures of Superman* came on at the same time. At times, I would play sick just to watch the *Man of Steel.* However, the best part of having a church so close was baptisms. Yes, baptisms. As in the Mexican culture, the godparents, known as *nino* and *nina,* walked out after the baptism and threw *bolo,* or pockets full of coins, to all the kids waiting at the bottom of the stairs. We dove for quarters, nickels, and dimes. Sometimes we would have over one dollar's worth of change. I remember telling Chris this tradition, and she thought that was crazy coming from Oklahoma, of course.

My brother and I would proceed to Lupe's Market to spend our fortune on *The Days of Marvel* comic books and my favorite, *Archie.* The penny candies were a great deal, as were the baseball cards with gum, wax bottle candy, and tootsie rolls. And that summer, stickers came out—flower power stickers and The Munsters' and Adams Family cards and gum. It was a gold mine as far as I was concerned. As we got home, I missed the wide-open spaces of Okieville and asked if I could spend the rest of my summer there.

After two weeks, Grandma Hernandez picked me up, and I got to take my new stingray bike. I couldn't wait to show my cousins on my mom's side and my buddies Rich and Steve, as well as my best buddy Chris. She had a purple boy's stingray and, of course, could outride anyone. What they didn't have was a small flower power sticker on the back of their bike. Yep, I'm a weirdo.

Besides the rural feel of Okieville, I had my own room in my grandparent's home, unlike Colton, where we shared a room with an uncle as my brother and I slept on bunk beds. I also decorated my room with blacklight posters of Jimmy Hendrix and a pirate's ship. I loved my space.

I couldn't wait to unload my slick bike and roam the streets of Okieville. After getting my clothes—shorts and t-shirts—into my room, I asked my grandmother if I could go to a friend's house. I would stop by Steve and Bobbie's house on the way to see Chris.

First, I collected empty Coke and 7-Up bottles to take to Jim's Market down the street to get our 5 cents to purchase a fresh Coke or ice cream, depending on the mood. It was hot that day. As I rode up to the store, I saw Chris' shiny purple bike parked in front. I couldn't wait to show off my new stingray. As she walked out with a coke bottle in hand, I couldn't help to feel my heart flutter for a minute. What was that? I thought. The feeling quickly left when she said, "Hey Anthony, you need a haircut. When did you get back?" Of course, the rage for me was The Beatles, and I wanted long hair like everyone else in the world.

I quickly grabbed a Coke, and we were off riding the streets of Okieville. Chris was on her way to visit my cousin, Zona, as they had become pretty good friends. I tagged along as I wanted to say hello as well. My cousin lived a few blocks over, and when we arrived, she was out front talking with the other kids in the neighborhood. As we rode up, I took this opportunity to show off my riding skills. I popped a wheelie and fell straight back. So much for that, *boys.*

Chris and I were happy to see each other. We talked about the Baker brothers, who had moved onto one of the fields down San Bernardino Avenue, and farmers from Oklahoma—Clyde and Jessie—who were put in our grade but looked like they belonged in Junior High. They were strong and not too smart at the same time, but for sure, they were bullies!

My first encounter with the Baker brother Jess was during a school softball game. They weren't really good athletes but strong and mean. Once, I made the mistake of laughing at Jess. He ran towards me and grabbed me by the neck, lifting me off the ground with my feet dangling. Thanks to a friend named Debbie, who I believed Jess had a crush on, she yelled at him to let me go, and he did. From that day forward, I stayed as far away from him as I could. Well, apparently, they were caught stealing candy and cigarettes at the new *Circle K* that had just opened next to our school. They were definitely the *bad boys* of the neighborhood. They spent two days in Juvenile Hall and were now back on the streets bullying anyone in their way, trying to act tough.

"Maybe I should teach them a lesson," I said.

Everyone looked at me and shook their heads, and advised me to stay away. Of course, Chris said, "You'll get your skinny butt kicked." She was probably right, as I was all of 100 pounds soaking wet.

That being said, summer in Okieville started out to be a great time. It was filled with trips to the wash, jumping off the railroad bridge, making softball fields on my grandparents' land, and late at night with my cousins playing 45 records and listening to the planes at Norton Air Force Base, which was located right behind our property line.

Let me tell you a little about the Hernandez property. My grandfather built his first house on the corner of San Bernardino Avenue and Mt. View. He purchased six lots after that, and all the homes and land were family-owned. He was one of the hardest-working men I have ever met in my life.

I recall at one point that summer Grandpa Hernandez was working not one, not two, but three jobs. At a local lumber company, a dairy, and for a citrus farmer. One of my fondest memories was my grandpa coming home after his first job in his worn-out white Chevrolet pickup truck. He would park in the driveway, and we would all come out to see him. He would sit in the cab of his truck with the Dodger game on and Vince Scully announcing the game. We would jump in as my grandma would bring him dinner in a brown paper bag to take to his next job. As Grandpa Hernandez sat there, he would take out his *Prince Albert* can of tobacco and roll up a cigarette. To this day, I can still smell it as he lit it up. We would then talk about our day, baseball, and anything else we had on our minds. I couldn't have asked for a better grandpa. I truly believe he is where I got my work ethic!

Well, the summer flew by, and we were all looking forward to the Sixth and last grade of elementary school. I was very excited to sport my new bell bottom cords, blue and brown, of course, and my new Nehru shirt. I thought I was Paul McCartney, but not so much. I heard I was going to be in Mr. Anderson's class—a fun teacher—with my best friend, Christine.

Chapter 8

I was excited about the last day of school, but I also was down as my dad had moved back, and his intention was to move the family back to Oklahoma. I was praying my mom was strong enough to say no. On this day, it was going to be all about having fun with the annual softball game against the teachers, and my best friend Anthony had promised me some flower power stickers, like the kind on the TV show *Laugh-In*, that they only sold in the store in South Colton where his other grandma lived.

I was always impressed with how Anthony bounced between his grandparents' homes during the school year but loved the summer as he spent most of it in Okieville. As I turned the corner on my way to school, there was Anthony and his buddies coming up the dirt path. As always, Anthony had his tin Batman lunch box open, eating a twinkie for breakfast. As my brothers ran off ahead of me, I waited for my best friend. Anthony had already made the line-up for the traditional softball game and had me playing shortstop.

The day started like all other days, saying the Pledge of Allegiance to start the day in class, and then it was time to have fun. The softball game was magical. I had at least half the outs and hit a home run over poor Mrs. Swan's head. She was a great

Fifth Grade teacher and college athlete but slipped as she went for the ball. The score at the time was 5-5 in the last inning, and with that shot, we made history, beating the teachers 6-5.

After the game, I was named M.V.P. Anthony was so excited that he threw his glove in the air before running toward me and spinning me around like a top. Speaking of tops, I sure loved mine! We all had a picnic lunch after the game and before we headed into our last class in elementary school. As the last bell ended our great day, Anthony handed me a pack of *flower power* stickers as he said he would. I would cherish them forever and put them up in my room in the future. I'm not sure what room or where, but at that time, it didn't matter.

As we walked home, I told Anthony we should have a Santa Ana River day when he comes back for the summer. He agreed and called me Jack Snow, and said he couldn't wait until we got to Junior High School. Little did I know that was the last day I would see Anthony Garcia, my best friend.

When I got home, the living room was filled with moving boxes. I couldn't believe my eyes, and my brothers looked like they had just seen one of my models of Frankenstein staring at them. I ran back to school, where my mom, the PTA President, was selling popsicles.

As I approached, my mom said, "You just missed your friend Anthony and his brother. They bought two popsicles, and I believe their father picked them up as I recognized his Pontiac GTO, you know, the one that looks like the Batmobile."

I sighed and said, "Mom, are we moving?"

"We would talk when we got home."

While I was waiting for my mom to finish packing, I realized that not only was I not looking forward to our conversation at home but also that my best friend had left for his other grandma's place, and I had no idea when he would return.

When we got home, my mom sat my brothers and me down and explained we would be moving back home to Oklahoma, as Dad had a job there and he wanted to be closer to family. I said what about school and my friends here. I was so looking forward to going to Junior High here, and it wasn't fair! I protested as a typical pre-teen would. And then, I finally said it. "What about Dad's drinking and his abuse?" At that moment, my father walked in with a six-pack of beer from Jim's Market and a pack of Marlboros. As he stumbled in, I asked to be excused, and after a tongue-lashing by Dad for not doing the dishes, I escaped on my bike—the purple stingray I loved more than him.

As I rode, I went by Anthony's grandparents' house, and

there was no sign of Anthony or his brother. My mom was right. His dad had picked him up and taken him to the other side of the world, Colton, California. I prayed he would come back before we moved. But that wouldn't happen. When I returned home, there was a huge U-Haul truck in our driveway.

I kept riding by the house and decided to go see my friend, Zona, as she was close to being with Anthony as she was his cousin. As I approached, I saw her outside on her front porch.

"Zona, do you have time to go for a bike ride?"

"Sure, let's go to the new Circle K. It's hot out, and they have these cool drinks called Slurpees, in cherry and coke flavor."

Off we went flying on our *boys* bikes down the street, past our school, and over the railroad tracks. We parked our bikes out front, and we both got a coke-flavored Slurpee, a bag of taco-flavored Doritos, and a can of Frito Lay bean dip. We sat in front of the store, and for one moment, life was good.

"Zona, I'm really upset as my family is moving back to Oklahoma, my father hasn't changed, and I don't want to go."

"I'm sorry to hear that, but family is a priority. We can always stay in touch by writing letters, and who knows, maybe when you get older, you'll move back to California."

I told Zona I was going to hate it and I would miss her and her cousin, Anthony, my best friend. Just then, it hit me that he was more than that, and I confessed to Zona that I believed I liked Anthony as a boyfriend. I was crushed I couldn't see him that day. Zona assured me she would let Anthony know, and perhaps he would be back before she moved.

We finished our treats, and I gave Zona a hug and told her I would always remember her. After that, we both rode our separate ways. I rode back home and found my brothers outside, not happy at all. They told me Dad was angry and took off to *Joe's bar* down the street and said we better be packed when he got home. Mom was inside, getting our clothes out, and making dinner.

"I'm not going anywhere," I told my brothers and rode off. I wasn't sure where I was going, but it didn't matter until I came upon the Baker boy bullies, Clyde and Jessie.

Jessie was the older *hick* and called out to me, "Hey, Bozo, where are you riding off to? Your boyfriend Anthony isn't around to protect you."

I never liked being pushed around and was in no mood, so I rode straight up to them and slid, spraying dirt on their already dirty clothes. Jessie then grabbed me by the hair, pulling me off my bike and throwing me on the ground. Both he and his brother

Clyde then proceeded to jump on the banana seat of my stingray and rode off, stealing the only possession of mine I truly loved.

I got up and dusted myself off, not sure what to do. If I went home and told my dad, he would most likely beat me for allowing that to happen, as he was as big a bully as the Baker boys. I dusted off my shorts and went home. I decided to tell my parents my bike was stolen at Circle K. That didn't go well at all. I was told to go out and find my bike as my dad was sure it was taken by a local kid. I left the house and walked over to the silos where I spent time when I needed to be alone. As I sat there, my brothers showed up and said they would help me look for my bike. I told them what really happened, and they both wished Anthony and his brother, Artie, were here as they were sure they could round up their friends and cousins to get my bike back. I told them it was okay, and I'll wait and hope we don't move for a few weeks.

However, my wish never came true, we were moving in two days, and it was then that I decided to run away. I went into my room and waited until it was late and everyone was asleep. I only took the clothes on my back and took one of the flower stickers Anthony gave me and put that in my pocket. My goal was to run to Anthony's grandma's house in Colton, about ten miles away. As I snuck out of the house, I could hear the big C141 plane engines warming up at Norton Air Force Base and the crickets as loud as a Beatle song I had heard once, but I would miss all of this.

I decided to wake up my friend Zona and headed to her house to let her know my plans. As I arrived, the house was dark, and I decided to leave her a note in her basket on her Schwinn bike.

Dear Friend,

I know what you said about family, but I just can't leave this place. I love my school and friends, and my father is evil. I'm going to try and hide until they leave. I'll try and get a hold of you tomorrow. Thank you for being my friend!

Christine

I then decided I was exhausted, so I thought I would head to my sanctuary to get some sleep before I headed out of Okieville. The silos were secure and safe and a great place to get some rest. There was hay on the ground, and this helped as I lay down to sleep.

Chapter 9

I, Detective Dean Liter, grew up in the Sheriff's Department and worked my way up through working the jail and patrol. I was now the lead detective in one of the top homicide units in the nation at the San Bernardino County Sheriff's Department.

I served in the U.S. Marine Corp. and loved playing golf as well as beer and whiskey in my downtime; what little downtime I had.

The Sheriff's Department had the homicide unit broken up into teams. I was the leader of Team 1 and had two other detectives assigned to the team. Detective Mike Jones was a year from retirement and had a great deal of experience in solving murder cases. Detective Sandy Smith was the only female detective in the unit and was excellent in the area of forensic technology.

As I gathered the team in place, I felt fortunate to have such a good relationship with my partners. Deputy D.A. Garcia, who we called Tony, and I had recently concluded a one-year trial together, so we were aware of the amount of effort and attention to detail Tony demanded from us. At the same time, Tony worked all hours of the day and night preparing a case for trial.

The last case was the murder of a couple on vacation in the San Bernardino County Mountain range. It was a very difficult case that was ten years old by the time we had the evidence to finally solve it. Through the efforts of my partners, we put a circumstantial evidence case in place and used the tool of a *wiretap* to finally arrest, charge, and convict the suspect. I should note a *wiretap* of an individual's phone has to be supported with probable cause and exhaustion of all other attempts to get evidence on the suspect. At the time we got the wiretap, we *shook the tree,* meaning we did an act to get the suspects talking again after ten years, in this case, a search of the business. It worked because we overheard the murderer say, "The sheriff's detectives are *on our ass* again, and I hope they don't find my DNA from the crime scene." Well, we didn't, but that statement and all the other circumstantial evidence we had was enough for Tony, our hard-charging Deputy D.A., to file the case. It was a long and tough trial with numerous witnesses, but we were successful, and the defendant was sent to Death Row. We loved working with Tony as he was a *Fighter Pilot* who fought hard during trials but could also relax when the battle was completed. So we were more than ready to work with him on this cold case.

This case was over thirty years old, and we were about to solve the oldest puzzle in the history of our department. The first task was to interview anyone that last had contact with Christine

Stone, which wouldn't be easy, but we started from a list of folks from Okieville, and from there, we would move on to Oklahoma.

We looked up all the friends and schoolmates that Tony had listed for us, including the last places Christine was seen in Okieville. Our first stop was Tony's cousin, Zona. She still resided in Okieville, in fact, lived in the house that her grandparents built on San Bernardino Avenue. She was now a teacher and continued to stay in touch with her cousin, Tony.

As we approached the house, we saw how time had changed this rural town, from mostly agriculture to tilt-up buildings and four-lane roads that were once a nice, peaceful thorough way between Redlands and San Bernardino. Years later (in 2015, to be precise), two local terrorists would be shot and killed on San Bernardino Avenue after attacking and murdering twelve people and injuring numerous individuals at a County Christmas gathering. To this day, one of the worst terrorist attacks in the country.

Zona invited us in and offered us some coffee which we gladly accepted. I asked Zona about the last time she saw her friend Christine.

"It was the last day of school and... forgive me, but I still get emotional about Christine. I prayed she would come back. In fact, I thought she would end up back East running a huge business. I'm sure she would've been successful, no matter what she did.

Anyway, as I said, I saw her on the last day of school. She was upset that her parents, out of nowhere, decided to move back to Oklahoma. This was after her dad moved back, which she was not happy about. We rode our bikes down to the new Circle K, and after getting some Slurpees, we sat down and had a long talk. To this day, I feel bad because I told her family came first and that she should go. I didn't know how abusive her father was until I learned she had gone missing. I later found a note she left me, and I wish to this day she would have woken me up."

"Was that the last time she contacted you?"

"Yes. I tried writing her family in Oklahoma, but they never returned my letters."

"Is there anything else you can remember that may be helpful?"

"Well, like I told investigators back in 1970, she was very close to my cousin, Anthony, who I'm sure you know, as I read in the newspaper, was assigned this case. And she was a *free bird* and loved open spaces, especially the Santa Ana River and the silos and wheat fields.

The one thing she despised were the Baker brothers, Clyde and Jessie, who had moved to Okieville the summer before. They were bullies, and it's my understanding that they stole her *stingray,* the bike she loved, and assaulted her. I told this to the detectives in 1970 as well. I still can't wrap my head around the fact that her family moved weeks after she went missing. How could they leave a daughter behind like that?"

"Well, Zona, that's what we intend to find out. Thank you for your time, and if you can think of anything else, please contact us."

"Wait, one more thing, I received a flower sticker in my mailbox the other day. The same kind of old stickers we loved in 1969. I thought it was odd and a sick joke."

"Do you still have it?"

"Yes."

"Can we take the envelope and sticker?"

"Sure thing."

As we left, Sandy and I looked at each other, and she gave me that *here we go* look. A good first step. Now, off to Oklahoma.

As we discovered, Mr. Stone had died of cirrhosis of the liver ten years ago. Mrs. Stone lived in a trailer park, and her two sons were living not far from her.

When we got back to the office, there was a message from Forensic Anthropologist Anderson. The note said to call him back. It seemed he had some not-so-good news. I called him back and put the phone on speaker for the team to hear. Dr. Anderson answered with the flair of a mortician or the Addams Family butler, "You rang?" Literally, that's how he answered his phone! Dr. Anderson proceeded to give us the results of his findings.

"Well, team, whoever these bones belong to won't be easy to solve without some DNA or dental records of your missing person. The bones have deteriorated, as one can imagine. I can still say that they are of a person somewhere in the adolescent years of 10-16 years, depending on the size of the individual. The clothing was also decomposed, and it could be argued the hole in the top was caused by that. The other news was the flower sticker was intact and was sent to the crime lab to see if we were lucky with fingerprints. This could be our last hope without DNA or dental records."

We thanked Dr. Anderson and told him we would hopefully get back to him with more evidence. I also ended the phone call with, "*Cousin Itt* would be all over this. Thanks, *Lurch.*" With that, we all laughed.

"You do have to have a sense of humor in this line of work," Sandy said.

We headed out to Oklahoma, hoping to find some more evidence that would solve this thirty-year-old puzzle. Mrs. Stone's trailer park was on the outskirts of Tulsa, Oklahoma. As we arrived, we noted how fast we went from some very nice neighborhoods with Oklahoma Sooner's flags hanging from their front porches to the poorest neighborhoods, which included the trailer park we were looking for.

Zona had given us the address where she mailed her letters, and Sandy used her technology skills to track down Mrs. Stone. As we approached her mobile home, I couldn't help but feel sorry for Christine's mother, now in her early 80s. As she answered the door, we displayed our badges and introduced ourselves as the homicide detectives working on the disappearance of her daughter. We did not want to use the term murder yet as we still had to prove the bones discovered were Christine's.

Mrs. Stone answered the door wearing a robe, as it was pretty early, and invited us in. She had just brewed a hot pot of coffee, and we never turned down a hot cup of java. She had read the newspaper from back home and asked if that was really her daughter.

"I was hoping she was alive and would someday knock on my door. I still hold out hope, but now I feel it slipping away."

I asked Mrs. Stone why they moved away shortly after her daughter went missing.

"Well, I didn't want to leave, but my husband said we don't know where she ran off to and said it was even possible that she came to Oklahoma to be with family. We had a huge argument, but in the end, he won, and we left. However, I did have the detective's card that was the lead on the search for Christine. However, my husband was really not happy with the Sheriff's Department."

"Why's that?"

"He said they treated him like a suspect after learning of his drinking habits and his abusive behavior."

"Did he ever physically abuse Christina?"

"There were two occasions where he would come home drunk and grab her or push her when he felt she was being disrespectful. The last time was the day she went missing. He became really upset about her bike being stolen. He blamed her."

"Do you believe he had anything to do with her missing?"

"I always had a part of me thinking he did something, but as you know, he is dead now."

"Do you have any of Christine's personal items? We were hoping to get DNA off of some of her items."

"I do not, as all it did was remind me of her. I only kept pictures."

No clothing, toothbrush, hairbrush, or any other items that could help us. A dead end. We then asked Mrs. Stone about dental records. She said she had not taken her kids to the dentist as they could not afford it.

"I tried to be the best mother I could with our low income. Instead of the dentist, we bought them bikes or footballs. She was never into dolls and loved sports."

At this time, Mrs. Stone lowered her head and started to cry. We asked her about where we could find Christine's brothers, Johnny and Bobby, and she said they were a town over. Both worked for the University of Tulsa as security guards, and we could find them at work today.

As we left Mrs. Stone's mobile home, we couldn't help but feel bad for her, but we also felt like we had struck out. We would call Tony with the news, but first, we headed to where the brothers worked. They would be 43 years old now, and we were fortunate to find them this fast. We got to the huge campus, and as luck would have it, Bobby was working the front visitor's booth.

We introduced ourselves, and Bobby said, "I was expecting you. Let me get ahold of my brother, and we can meet in my office."

We sat down with the twins, and they confirmed all we knew about their years in Okieville. Dad was an alcoholic and abusive, and their sister stood up to him and protected them at times. I then asked about the day she went missing.

"Well, Christine was upset that we were going to move, and she made that known to Mom. Of course, Mom did whatever Dad said, and we had to move. Christine then took off on her bike, and the next time we saw her, she came home without the bike. We asked her what happened as she was upset, and she told us the Baker boys had taken her bike and assaulted her. To this day, I wish we had been there for my sister. Of course, she didn't tell our dad that, and she just said it was stolen at Circle K. He was not happy and sent her out to look for it. Sometimes I wonder if Dad had something to do with her disappearance, but we keep coming back to the Baker brother bullies. I truly believe one of them hurt our sister," Bobby recounted the story. "Are the bones recovered hers?"

"That's what we are trying to determine."

Johnny said, "I hope they are not hers as I want to believe she is alive and just changed her life, but I know she cared about our mother and us, and she would have never left us like that. I pray you arrest the person that killed our sister, and as Bobby said, my bet is one, or both, of the Baker boys."

"When was the last time you saw the Baker brothers?"

"When we moved from Okieville. I know the Sheriff's Deputies interviewed them years ago as they confronted us at *Jim's Market* and said if we sent the Deputies on their trail, they would make us pay! Again, they were jerks!"

As we left the brothers, we gave them our information and told them to contact us if they had any more information.

Our next stop was the Baker brothers.

Chapter 10

It was a super fun year, and except for the melting popsicles in my pockets, it was a great year. I looked forward to the summer before going to Junior High School. In fact, after discussing it with my dad, Grandma Garcia, and Grandma Hernandez, I was going to stay in Okieville not only through the summer but during the school year. I was excited and looked forward to not feeling like a ping-pong ball bouncing between homes on a daily basis. It was two weeks later that Grandpa Hernandez picked me up, and I moved all I had with me, my clothes and my stingray. I was looking forward to a fun summer, and I couldn't wait to see my best friend, Christine.

Before Grandpa Hernandez rolled up, Grandma made us some burritos to go. That's how she was. She loved feeding people. After they exchanged hellos in Spanish, I jumped in the truck, and we headed to *wonderland,* as I thought of it. However, on the ride, my grandfather had some bad news.

"Anthony, your good friend, Christine, went missing. She hasn't been seen since the last day of school, and everyone has been looking for her."

I couldn't believe my ears.

"What?! Where are her parents and brothers? Did she run away?"

Grandpa took a drag off his rolled cigarette and said, "I'm not sure, but the community has come together to help look for her." He also said something I'll never forget. "As you know, her father isn't the friendliest person in the world. He blames everyone for her going missing. In fact, he spends all day at Joe's Bar while others are searching for his daughter. Also, they just moved away yesterday. I heard Mrs. Stone was crying and totally depressed and was drugged into the moving van."

What kind of person does that? I was in shock at that point.

As we arrived, I unloaded my bag of clothes and went into the room Grandma had set up for me. It did feel so good to have my own room. In fact, a week prior, I had gone to the Colton Auction and purchased a couple of black light posters and a small black light lamp. I was going to have a cool room. I also had a small record player and couldn't wait to spin The Beatles' "Sgt. Pepper's Lonely Hearts Club Band" on it, as it was *wonderful to be here.*

After I unpacked, I jumped on my bike and rode off, not knowing where I was going, but the first thing I saw was Christine's picture on a poster attached to a telephone pole. A missing poster with her date of birth and a number to call if someone saw her or had any information. My heart sank.

I rode up and down the streets, from Mt. View to Cooley Avenue, up Victoria Avenue, stopping at the silos where I knew Chris loved to run off to and hide. I sat there for a half hour or so and looked around for any signs of her. After seeing none, I decided to ride over to Cousin Zona's house.

As I rode over the bridge, I had to stop and take in my old school, Victoria Elementary. Such good memories, but as much as I would miss the great teachers I had, I was looking forward to moving on. I got to Zona's house, and my Aunt Tense answered the door. It was good to see her, and she invited me in for some of her great homemade cookies as she let Zona know I was there.

We sat at the kitchen table and talked about our friend Christine and all the special moments we had with her. Zona thought for sure she ran away and, knowing her, probably hitchhiked her way across the country.

"I spoke with Sheriff Detectives several days ago, and I told them the same thing. She was upset her family was moving and was really going to miss you, Anthony. In fact, I truly believe she had feelings for you, and I thought maybe she ran away to see you."

I told Zona she did not come to see me and was surprised detectives did not interview me.

"I did get a note from her, and she said that she loved her school and friends and that her father was evil. She said she was going to try and hide until they left and said she would try to get ahold of me the next day. I never heard from her again."

After catching up, I rode back to Grandma's house, passing Chris' house again on Victoria Avenue. On my way back, I ran into one of my classmates, Johnny Perez. He asked if I had heard about Chris, and he went on to tell me what he had heard about the Baker brothers.

"Did you hear that the brothers stole her bike and pushed her down while taking it? I can't help to think one of those bullies caused her to run away or, even worse, did something to her after that."

"Has anyone seen them since she went missing?"

"I have not, but the word on the street is that the detective interviewed them, but they were not arrested."

"What about Christine's bike?"

"It has not been found, and everyone was looking for that as well."

I rode my bike back home and couldn't help to think if I had been here, Chris would have come to me, and everything would be okay. I was sure she would be found. She had big dreams, and I was sure she left to chase those dreams, but where?

That summer was one of the best ever. I heard the Baker brothers were sent back to Oklahoma for the summer, and I hoped they never returned. The thing about summers in Okieville was the days were long, and there was plenty to do. For instance, playing softball games with family in the field next to Grandma's house and Grandpa Hernandez pitching for both teams and playing *Army* with my cousins. *Combat* with Vic Morrow was a great show, and I always wanted to be the Sargent. I even made a roller coaster out of orange crates and plywood, with a wagon I would pull my younger cousins on. Of course, I got in trouble for that one. One tip over and Grandpa's good wood didn't go over too well. I had my first job painting a patio for a friend of one of my aunts, and I used the money I made to buy my first guitar. The first song I learned was "Hey Jude" by the Beatles, and I must have played that a thousand times that summer.

The summer flew by, and I thought about Chris every day. I was excited to go to Junior High School, but I would truly miss my best friend. I swore to myself that I would never forget her and when I got older, I would find her wherever her life had taken her.

My years in Junior High flew by. My buddies and I started a garage band called *Mighty Mighty,* playing songs like Steve Miller Band's "The Joker." I loved the line: *I really love your peaches want to shake your tree.* Little did I know that term would come back to me in the future as a prosecutor—*shaking the tree*—during a wiretap. Of course, that's not what we were thinking at the time. It was just adolescent juices flowing.

However, sports were still my number one extracurricular activity. I was on the track team, undefeated, running the 660-yard race, played guard on the basketball team, second string, and was a wide receiver on the football team. Every time I lined up in that position, I thought of the Ram's *Jack Snow* and my own Jack Snow in elementary school, Christine. I wish she could be here now.

However, it was the summer before the 9th Grade that really molded me for what I would do for my professional future. I was down the street from my house with a good friend Jimmy. As we were walking, two local gang members approached us and asked what we were doing in their neighborhood. Being the person I was, I said, "I don't see any signs that say you own these streets." One of them proceeded to approach me and poked a switchblade knife into my chest. "You need to join the gang," he said. I responded, "I already have friends and family." He proceeded to push the blade into my chest, wanting me to move or run. I didn't, and the blade penetrated my t-shirt and slightly cut my skin as the tip of the blade cut me. He then looked scared and withdrew the knife, and ran away with his buddy.

I looked at Jimmy, and he said, "Let's go, Anthony. We can get them back in the future."

Little did I know, the future would come years later when the two gang members were prosecuted in an undercover operation and were sent to prison.

This incident made me who I am today, a fighter for victims' rights. I certainly know what it feels like to be victimized! I also was a fighter and was in two after-school fights as I refused to be bullied by older students. My dad, the former Marine, made me tough, along with my life in Okieville. Bring it on!

High School was some of the best years of my life. I had left our band and focused on sports, specifically football… *Terrier Football,* to be precise. Redlands High School was a great school and a football powerhouse. I loved the game. To this day, our Junior Varsity team holds the record of not only being undefeated, but no one scored a point on us! I was a *free safety* and *wide receiver* on that team. I became a *varsity starter* my senior year, and there was nothing like Friday nights. We were the stars of the community. Our coach wore white shoes, and they called him *White Shoes.* He was an excellent coach, and he helped shape me into the man I am today.

The year was 1975, and we played against two future pro football Hall of Famers, Ronnie Lott and Anthony Munoz. We beat both of their teams, 35-0 and 27-7, respectively. Our quarterback was as good as any in the country. In fact, he got a full scholarship to Arizona State, playing for Frank Kush, who had a great program, one of the best in the nation, but was a tough coach. As for me, I played *running back (RB)* in 1975 and *split-side defensive end.* A 5'7" and 150-pound Defensive End. I was not big at all, but I could bench press 250 pounds and run the 40-yard dash in 4.6 seconds, not bad for a skinny brown kid.

However, the best thing that happened to me was meeting the girl I would marry and spend my life with. She was a knockout with long brown hair. Rachel Irey was smarter than me and was a student body leader and a homecoming princess. We had so many good times, and we were named the best couple in our senior year. We had the same goals, a college education, and a family. She is the reason I became a lawyer and prosecutor. To this day, she remains my right-hand person. We did have two kids, Christine Michele and Patrick Michael, and I bring this up as they both attended Victoria Elementary School, where I attended with Christine. As I said before, I will never forget Christine, and I thought the best way to fight crime—always loved that Batman lunch pail—was to become a prosecutor.

After getting an undergraduate degree from the University of California at Riverside, Rachel and I married in 1981. I became a Probation Officer with the San Bernardino County Probation Department, where I met one of my best friends, Barry Truman, who has since retired and is the author of a great book, *Search Me*.

Our daughter was born in 1983, and it was then I decided I wanted to go to law school. There was a part-time law school in Riverside County, where I attended night classes for four years. After passing the California Bar Exam, one hell of a three-day test, I knew the only thing I wanted to practice was being a prosecutor. It was in my blood. I now look back, and I see where my passion for victims comes from. Being bullied myself and my mother's death.

I vowed to fight for victims for the rest of my life!

Chapter 11

The Baker brothers, we discovered, had moved right after Christine went missing. We pulled the original interviews out of the cold case file. Both Clyde and Jessie denied ever seeing Christine on the last day of school, and their parents, Mr. and Mrs. Baker, were adamant that the boys never left the farm. The detectives asked if they could look around the farm as Christine's bike was missing. They refused to consent to a search warrant. As the detectives left the farm, they could observe several bikes in the backyard area, one appearing to be purple in color. With the information they gathered from Johnny and Bobby Stone, they had slim probable cause for a search warrant. But this was a huge case of a missing girl, and the judge signed the warrant. The detectives returned a day later, and after serving the search warrant, they discovered the purple bike was missing. Of course, all of the Baker Family members denied ever having such a bike. The only piece of evidence found was an open package of *flower power* stickers that Christine's brothers had indicated were hers. With no other information, they closed the file on the Baker boys. It was time for our team to follow up.

Sandy went to work on tracking the Baker family down. We discovered the parents were now deceased. Clyde Baker was now in State Prison in Chino, California, for a list of felonies, his last one a kidnap for a rape conviction, and Jessie was in the wind. Clyde was also a member of a local outlaw motorcycle gang, The Loco's, a gang whose members we had prosecuted before and who hated Deputy District Attorney Garcia because, at one press conference, he called them *local terrorists.* They despised him for that. We learned that the current gang leader was Clyde's right-hand man in many of the drug-related charges he was convicted of. He had served as the best man at Clyde's wedding as well. His name was Peter Ramirez, and he was feared by many. As for Clyde's wife, she was dead after a *biker* shootout in a Laughlin Casino. These folks were dangerous! We did discover Clyde had a daughter who still lived in Okieville, and we put her on our list to interview. Her name was Debbie Baker.

We first visited Chino State Prison. We intended to question Clyde once again and confront him with what we thought were Christine's remains. As we entered the visiting room, Clyde was tatted up from head to toe and was not very happy to see us. We introduced ourselves, and I told him we just wanted to talk about Christine Stone and her disappearance.

To our surprise, Clyde talked to us about his younger years.

"I don't know what the hell happened to Christine, but I can tell you that was a long time ago. My brother and I moved to

Okieville with our horrible parents and hated it there. Too many Mexicans and *sweet Polly purebreds.*"

"Do you remember Christine?"

"Yes, she was one of those that thought she was all that and a bag of chips, and her boyfriend at the time was a punk by the name of Anthony. I'm sure you know him as he is a prosecutor now and has helped put many of my friends in prison. He's an asshole and is not liked by my brothers."

"You mean your gang brothers?"

"Whatever you want to call them, but what does that have to do with anything over thirty years ago? I had nothing to do with that tomboy's disappearance."

"A purple bike was seen at your old house back then. What happened to that?"

"I don't know what you're talking about. We couldn't afford fancy bikes."

"Do you recall a package of what has come to be known as *flower power* stickers?"

"Hell no, do I look like a girl to you?"

"What about your brother, Jessie?"

"What about him?"

"Did he take a bike from Christine or have stickers he may have taken from her?"

"Why don't you ask him? Good luck with that."

That summer, Clyde then told us, his asshole parents (as he referred to them) moved and left them to fend for themselves. They went back to Oklahoma, and he and his brother ended up in foster homes.

"I haven't seen Jessie since. The last I heard, he became a fisherman of all things and was out in the ocean doing his thing."

"Your parents are both now deceased. Did you have any contact with them after they abandoned you?"

"No!"

"One final question, did you steal Christine's bike and physically assault her the summer after 6th Grade?"

"No, and hell no. Tell that Mexican prosecutor he's barking up the wrong tree."

"How do you know who's on this case?"

"I read the papers in here, and he is on a wild goose chase. Good luck with that. I have nothing more to say."

With that, the guards opened up the doors to the interview room and let us out. On the way to our vehicle, we all agreed Clyde was lying and that we needed to talk with anyone he communicated with. Our next stop was Peter Ramirez, the leader of The Loco's Motorcycle Gang.

We did some background checks on Ramirez and found out that he grew up in Okieville, down the street from the Baker brothers. He spent a lot of his younger years in Juvenile Hall, starting at age 13. His criminal record reached the floor. He was mostly convicted of narcotics sales and various assault and battery charges. Ramirez started the motorcycle gang in his early twenties and, by all indications, recruited Clyde Baker, who Sheriff's intel had listed as the secretary of The Loco's gang.

Deputy DA Garcia, Tony, knew Ramirez as well, saying he at one time was assaulted by him in Junior High but left it at that. Tony did say Ramirez was part of the bullies that terrorized the streets of Okieville when growing up, but he was not around much as he was often living in Juvenile Detention Camps while Tony enjoyed great years in school.

As luck would have it, Peter was sitting in our local County Jail on another drug charge. Our plan was to discuss his relationship with the Baker brothers, especially with Clyde indicating his dislike for Mexicans, which we found very interesting.

As Peter walked into the interview room, he stated, "What now?"

We told Ramirez we wanted to talk to him about growing up in our county as we were doing research on his motorcycle gang.

Ramirez laughed at us and said, "They aren't a gang and, in fact, are just guys with families that enjoy riding as a hobby and a love for motorcycles."

"What about Clyde Baker?"

"What about him?"

"Did you know him growing up?"

"Yes, but so what?"

"Did you know a girl by the name of Christine Stone?"

"No, and I'm done talking to you."

"Why?"

"I heard she went missing years ago, and I can see now you're trying to implicate my *homie, Clyde.*"

"How do you know that?"

"Fuck you. I'm done!"

Well, that interview didn't go well, but we expected as much.

Our next stop was a trailer park in Okieville at the corner of San Bernardino Avenue and Mt. View Avenue, across the street from the first house Tony's grandfather built and caddy corner to an Edison plant. Debbie Baker lived there, and we were surprised that a mobile home park still existed with all the *tilt-up* industrial buildings across the street.

The next morning, we approached her mobile home. Several hungry-looking dogs started barking at us, and I knew just what to do. I always carried dog treats in my *man purse.* " I fed dogs on the golf course, so why not when I'm out working? They quickly become your friends, and true to form, it worked. We knocked on the door, and a woman with a toddler in her arms answered with not a hello, but a W.T.F. I decided to let Sandy take the lead on this one, female to female, you see.

We had sent Mike to get the phone records from Chino State Prison and County Jail pertaining to Peter Ramirez and any communications he had with Clyde Baker. Believe it or not, this is still allowed, as there is a warning that all phone conversations must be recorded and may be used against you unless you are talking to your attorney. You would be amazed at how many inmates spilled their guts on a recorded phone call. However, we weren't sure about these two career criminals. But we had to give it a shot. My partner, Sandy, was as smooth as they came. She was an *all-world* soccer player at the University of Redlands, and along with her technical skills, she could out-charm a snake charmer.

"May we come in? I'm Detective Sandy Smith, and this is my partner, Detective Dean Liter. I know he looks scary with his goatee, but he is a pushover for kids and dogs, for that matter."

Thanks… was not what went through my brain.

Debbie looked at both of us and said, "Sure, come in." She yelled at an older sibling to come and hold the baby sister. "Have a seat. Sorry about the mess, but it's hell being a single mom with three kids running wild."

We sat at a small kitchen table, and thank God I had boots on as I stepped on several Legos.

"What is it you want with me? Is my ex-husband in trouble, or is it about my dad again?"

"It's about your father," Sandy said.

"What did he do now?"

It was obvious Debbie was very comfortable talking with Sandy and kept giving me the evil eye. Maybe I should shave, I thought.

Sandy was very smooth. "We would like to talk about your relationship with your father to start with."

"Well, as I'm sure you know, my dad was in and out of jail for most of my life, and because of his membership to that gang he belongs to, it resulted in my mom being killed in the crossfire. Her killer has never been caught. To this day, I blame my dad."

"Do you still communicate with him?"

"Yes, at times, he calls me from prison. I think on a burner phone, but our conversations are more about the kids. I refuse to take them to prison."

"When you were younger, where did you live?" Sandy inquired.

"Right here. My grandparents dumped my father and uncle, whom I've never met. This is the same mobile home I grew up in. It really wasn't a bad place to grow up. They have great schools here, and before all the industrial box warehouses, it was a place to escape into the wheatfields and orange groves that stretched all the way down San Bernardino Avenue. Now all of that is almost gone."

"Growing up here, did you hear about the missing young girl, Christine Stone, who went missing over thirty years ago?"

"Why? Yes, my mom told me about her when I would stay out late with my friends or wouldn't come home until the next day. She would say, 'Do you want to end up like that Christine girl?' My teenage years were all about big parties. I'm paying for that now... three kids and on welfare."

"Did your father ever talk about her? We understand that they went to school together."

"Not really."

"What do you mean?"

"He would only shake his head when Mom would make those comments about Christine, but I do remember one time him saying, 'She probably got what she deserved.'"

"What did he mean by that?"

"I don't know, as I was being yelled at by my mother. I never asked him. You don't think my dad had something to do with her disappearance, do you?"

"Not sure yet, but we have re-opened it as a *cold case,* and anything you can remember would be a great help," Sandy explained.

"Well, I know my dad is a crook, but he would never hurt anyone."

I then opened my mouth and said, "But you weren't around when your dad was in his teenage years."

"No kidding! I've had enough. Will you please leave now?"

Sandy gave me that *way to go* look and asked Debbie if she could ask her one more question.

"Sure, but I don't like your partner."

"Did you ever have a bike while growing up?"

"Yes, my dad gave me an old, cleaned-up Schwinn Stingray, I believe it was called. I loved my bike as it allowed me to escape this crazy house and ride forever."

"Can you give us details of your bike?"

Debbie looked at me and then back at Sandy and said, "It was purple in color, had a banana seat, and had a little flower sticker right below the handlebars."

"Do you still have it?"

"No, it fell apart years ago. Why?"

"Just curious, as I had an orange one growing up."

Sandy and I looked at each other and decided let's quit while we're ahead. As we left, we couldn't help but feel good about that interview. We got another part of the puzzle. We knew Tony would approve.

It was time to head back to the office and see what, if anything, Mike was able to get off the phone records. On the way back to the office, we stopped at a local Mexican takeout. Nothing like a garbage burrito to fill us up for what would be another long day. One of the great things about Southern California… Mexican food.

When we got to the office, Mike was sitting at his desk with his feet up and his hands behind his head. "Good to see you two. I hope you got me a taco or two?"

"We sure did," I replied.

After devouring our lunch, we got back to work.

Mike said we had one hit on the phones he looked into. "No phone use from Peter Ramirez at the jail in the last two days, at least not yet. But our friend, Clyde, made a call from the prison phone to his daughter, Debbie." He sat up and hit the play button on his computer.

"Hey Deb, it's Dad."

"Hello, Dad, what's up? The kids aren't here right now."

"Well, some detectives came to see me about that missing girl from years ago. I'm sure they will try and contact you, but that's okay as you don't know anything, right?"

"Dad, did you have something to do with that? I mean... that was years ago."

"Hell no, I don't kill girls, although she was a pain in the ass, and she thought she was all that. Your uncle and I couldn't stand her and all her friends. Anyway, if the detectives come by, don't say a word."

End of call.

"Well, that doesn't help much," I said.

"No, but this will," Mike replied. "It came in ten minutes ago. I have friends inside the prison."

"Hello Deb, it's Dad."

"Well, you were right. Two detectives came by this morning. One was really nice, and one was a jerk."

"What did they ask you?"

"General questions about you, and then they started asking about that Christine girl from way back. Of course, I knew nothing about that, and they left. That's it. Oh wait, the nice

detective asked me about the old bike you fixed up for me, you know… that purple stingray."

"What did you tell them?"

"Just that… how you fixed it up for me."

"Shit, way to go. I told you to keep your mouth shut!"

With that, Mike hung up the phone. As we could hear, Clyde was angry and practically yelling at Debbie. Note she never told him what she overheard years ago: *she got what she deserved.*

It was time to go see Tony.

Chapter 12

As we walked into the D.A.'s office in downtown San Bernardino, you couldn't help but wonder how all these lawyers worked in such an old building. As we walked up the back staircase to the third floor, where Tony's office was, we had to step over a homeless person asleep on the stairs. How in the hell Tony worked here was beyond me, but we sure loved the fighter he was, and we were going to need his passion more than ever on this case, a 33-year-old cold case.

***

As Liter and Sandy entered my office, I was surrounded by the old case file boxes.

"Come on in, team. I have been going over the original missing person reports and interviews. I was amazed at how many folks walked through the fields and silos without seeing a trace of a crime scene. I did note that the day before the search for Christine, the silos were filled a fourth of the way with processed wheat. The reports indicated no sign of the missing girl in this location or any other location, for that matter.

I see that her dad was a suspect at first but had alibis, where he was at home or Joe's Bar, that was confirmed. It still boggles my mind that they moved about two weeks after she went missing. I read all the interviews of those that last saw her, including my cousin, Zona, and the Baker boys. I saw pictures of the missing person flyer attached to telephone poles. Too bad we didn't have the social media abilities we have now.

"What, if anything, did you two find out?"

Liter presented the evidence up to this point. "The interview with Clyde Baker at the prison site gave us little if anything, but it did work to *shake the tree* as he did what we thought, calling his daughter Debbie Baker as soon as he could. Luckily, we got to her before his first call, and Mike, with his contacts, got the phone recording between Clyde and Debbie Baker. Sandy did a great job with Debbie Baker. Good thing she was the lead on that interview as I can come across as a hard ass at times, but she was great."

The detectives went over the facts they had gathered with me. I felt good about the bike and Clyde's statement at home years ago: *she got what she deserved.* They described the interviews in Oklahoma and told me that they didn't find anything about the personal items that Christine may have owned. They further told that Christine's brothers believed that the Baker brothers had something to do with her disappearance, but it was all speculative, except for what their sister told them about her bike being stolen and the assault by Jessie Baker.

They then played the phone call between Clyde and his daughter.

"That's a good start," I said.

"Oh, one more thing. Peter Ramirez was a dead end, but we are waiting for him to make a call to Clyde. However, he may not be that stupid, and he is due to be released from jail next week," Liter explained.

Now, it was time to visit Forensic Anthropologist Dr. Steven Anderson at the crime lab.

As we drove a few blocks to the crime lab, Liter, being his typical self, asked, "Hey Tony, you're getting some *boat docks?* Perhaps you should try some Rogaine."

"Very funny, Liter. Perhaps it's stress related to your investigation skills!"

"Time will tell, Tony; we will make this case."

The crime lab was located in trailers, or, I should say, mobile home structures. No, they were trailers. At least they were secure. Dr. Anderson walked in, ducking his head through the doorway. He was as tall as his deep voice. Liter couldn't get *Lurch* out of his head as he loved the *Addams Family,* but he suppressed his smile and said hello before re-introducing our team.

Dr. Anderson then asked what we had for him regarding identification purposes. I told him there were no dental records as the victim's mother confirmed they could not afford to take their kids to the dentist, so we had nothing to compare the teeth we had forensically.

"It gets worse, Doc. We have no personal items of Christine Stone, like a toothbrush or even a hairbrush, to get some DNA for comparison. Her mother got rid of all her items except for pictures."

"Well, that's a problem as we can't identify the identity of the bones except for some circumstantial evidence. For instance, the time frame by looking at the deterioration of the clothing, the age of the bones and their deterioration, and a flower sticker," Dr. Anderson said.

The doctor told us about what the future held as far as DNA was concerned. "With familial DNA, we would be able to compare the DNA in the bones we found, but that has not been scientifically approved at this point.[1]" He then talked about the density of the bones. The fact that they were buried for over

---

[1] Familial D.N.A. was approved by Governor Jerry Brown in 2008, to be used only as a last resort when all investigative angles have been exhausted.

thirty years made it much more difficult. He indicated the male bone mass is usually thicker than a female, and a female is much smoother, but that's at the peak of bone mass growth. "It's harder to say at the age we are talking about. An adolescent bone structure." And before we asked, he looked at me and said, "Men and women do have the same number of ribs, Tony."

I pretended I knew that. "HA! I guess that's an old wives' tale."

"Well, there you have it, we not only have no I.D., but we can't say with 100 percent certainty that it was a female."

Thank God for the flower power sticker, as the clothing didn't help much as Christine wore boys' P.F. Flyers. This I knew himself. As for the flower sticker, there were no fingerprints or anything physically that tied the sticker to the case except its circumstantial evidence puzzle piece.

"This may be as bad a murder case to prove with the victim never being found. The case just got tougher," I remarked.

We thanked Dr. Anderson and made our way back to the office. Just then, I had an idea. When we got back, we went over what we had, but more importantly, some unanswered questions. One, where was Jessie Baker? If we were to believe Clyde, he hadn't seen him since the brothers were split up into foster homes. We needed to contact anyone who may know where he was. So far, a dead end.

"It's a big ocean," Liter commented.

"Secondly, we need to do a full background on Peter Ramirez and his relationship with Clyde Baker. I do recall them being friends back when we were all in grade school. If he is getting out of jail, perhaps it's time to *tap* his phone," I said.

"I know what that means," Liter said. "It's time to write a search warrant."

"That's right, young man," Sandy said.

"I'm on it!"

Liter and Sandy had taken Clyde's cell phone number from his personal property in the jail after visiting him. It was on his booking sheet.

As we were about to split up, Mike said, "Hold on, folks. Just got a ding on my phone. It looks like the *Loco's* prez made a jail call to his partner, Clyde. Let me pull it up."

"Clyde, it's Pete. Homie, we need to talk. Some detectives came by asking about you know who. I didn't tell them shit, but it appears they are re-opening the case."

"I know. They came here to interview me and then hit up my daughter, who opened up her big mouth."

"I'm due to be released from custody tomorrow. Don't say another word on this jail phone. Keep the burner you have, and I'll call you from my cell phone in the next few days. We need to be damn careful."

End of call.

Well, that just gave us a big boost for our *probable cause* in our search warrant to show Peter Ramirez is, in fact, a possible suspect. He was interviewed in 1970 but denied knowing anything, and his parents covered for him.

"Tony, well, we have exhausted all other evidentiary leads, so I believe a judge will sign it. Fingers crossed," Liter said.

The detectives worked on the search warrant into the night, and as I had hoped, Superior Court Judge Lisa Warren signed it, and we would be up and running by morning. It was time to *shake the tree* one more time. I also hoped we would keep Judge Warren on this case as she was fair but as tough as they come being a former prosecutor herself.

Chapter 13

As Peter walked out of jail, he had his gang members pick him up. They were wearing their colors and enjoyed cruising up to the jail, where most of them had spent some time.

"Let's head back to the *house*." That was the gang's headquarters located in a small patch of orange groves that still existed. Peter lived there, and it was handed down to him by his parents after they had passed away. As he unpacked, he started reminiscing about the early years of his life.

Growing up was great in this area. Plenty of space to run and ride bikes, with no buildings anywhere to be found. Most of the kids I went to school with were okay, but I didn't like school much and couldn't wait for the summers. One summer before 5th Grade, I believe a *bad kid* or two moved into the neighborhood. They became good friends. Clyde and Jessie Baker felt the same way. In fact, I recall many days, skipping school and heading down to Randle's Market, a small store, where I would keep the owner's attention while Clyde and Jessie filled their pockets with large bags of Peanut M&M's and Bazooka bubble gum. Yes, our career as criminals started back then. We didn't know that we just wanted some goodies for our day hanging out down in the Santa Ana River. Oh, I can't forget the two cans of beer. It had a foul taste back then, but we drank it. No one wanted to act like a *punk*, and drinking beer made us feel cool. But when summertime came, it was time to really have fun and cause trouble.

I do remember the day Christine went missing. I ran into the Baker brothers as they left their trailer park, laughing and riding a new purple stingray I hadn't seen before, or at least not with them. I asked them, "Where did you get the new *ride.*" Jessie just looked at me and said, "We borrowed it from that *tom girl,* Christine. We shoved her off the bike and took it, well, borrowed it. We heard her old man was out looking for whoever stole the bike. We overheard our drunk Dad saying he heard it at Joe's Bar. I thought we would track her down and give her the damn bike back, plus it has a sissy flower sticker on it." It was then that we took off looking for her.

As we stopped at the new Circle K to get a Slurpee, we saw Cristine walking toward the silos, a block away from the store. We jumped on our bikes and rode toward her. She saw us and began to run. As we got closer, we jumped off the bikes and chased her. My intention at the time was only to scare her. But she was faster than us, and we all split up to try and surround her. As we trampled over dirt and tumbleweeds, I heard a scream and saw Christine laying on the ground next to a huge rock next to the silos. I looked around and saw Clyde and Jessie running away now, and I decided to do the same. As we got to the bikes, I asked what had happened. Clyde said, 'I don't know what you're talking about. Let's just get out of here!' The next day the entire community was looking for Christine as she went missing. I recall riding as fast as I could home.

Several weeks later, her family moved, and my buddies were abandoned and living in foster homes later that summer. It was the last time I saw Jessie Baker, and Clyde was in a home that allowed us to reconnect in Junior High School. Whatever happened, I know I didn't do a thing regarding that missing girl.

The next morning, I woke up with the intention of finding some work. There had to be some type of employment with all these warehouses popping up all around us like huge mushrooms. However, as I was drinking my coffee, a knock came on my door. As I looked out the window, it was the same damn detectives that came to see me in jail.

As I answered the door, I asked, "What now?"

The detective with the goatee asked if they could come in for a few minutes. I thought to myself, why not. My house was clean as far as I knew, as I had been in jail for almost a year.

Detective Liter started out by telling me it's best to come clean now as we have a body, and there is evidence that ties you to it.

"Listen, Peter. We know you were around Christine Stone when she went missing, as we have some evidence that ties you to her that day."

"What?" I said. "That's bullshit, as I had nothing to do with it. I know how you cops work, make crap up to scare someone into talking. As I told you before, I have nothing to say, and I had nothing to do with that girl's murder."

"Murder?" Sandy asked. "Who said she was murdered?"

At that, I said, "Unless you're here to arrest me, you need to leave."

***

As Sandy and I left Peter's place, I looked at Sandy and said, "I believe he will be making a call soon."

"Let's give Detective Jones a heads up," Sandy replied.

"Sure enough."

As we got back to the office, Mike was sitting in front of his computer. He looked at us and said, "It's on."

The call was *hot* [live] as we took a seat to listen in.

"Clyde, it's Peter. I'm glad you kept your burner phone. What the fuck, man? The cops came to see me and said they had evidence that tied me to that missing girl."

"Peter, they have nothing on you, don't sweat it."

"Well, what the hell did happen? I'm trying to clean up, and this doesn't help."

"Look, my brother and I tackled her, and we both took off. We then went back to take care of business, and you don't want to know about any of that."

"Did you do her in?"

"Well, let's just say my brother was the last to see her, but I may have helped a little. As I said before, she had it coming!"

"Shit, brother, you guys are crazy. No wonder your brother is out to sea somewhere. Well, I'll keep my mouth shut, but the heat is on."

With that, the phone call ended. We all knew we had just found a huge piece of the puzzle. It was time to pack up the case and deliver it to D.A. Tony. We would need to pay another visit to Peter as well, but the wire was good for thirty days, and we would sit on it and hope for more. The fact that detectives are allowed to make up evidence to get a suspect or witness to talk sure helped to *shake the tree.*

We worked late that night, taking shifts and watching Mike's computer for any live calls. I got home around midnight. My home was my escape, along with some mellow rock on the record player and a glass of Jameson's Whiskey. It was midnight, and I decided to call Tony as I figured he would be up. When he was preparing a case or in a trial, he was up all hours of the night. When he was out of a trial, he was in bed by 8:00 PM. This wasn't the case tonight.

"Tony?"

"Yes."

"It's Dean."

"What do you have for me?"

After I shared the phone call with Tony, I heard silence on the other end and then what I believed to be a fist hitting a desk, then came a loud, YES!

"Dean, your team is amazing. Bring in everything you have tomorrow, and let's see if we can put together a case. We may need to turn Peter Ramirez, but that won't be easy. See you tomorrow."

With that, I knew my golf round was out of the question, or perhaps I could squeeze it in later tomorrow. It's the only thing that kept me sane. Perhaps I'll get Tony out there with me, and we could work on the course. As they say, great moments or deals occur on the golf course. I called Tony back.

"Yes?"

"Let's meet on the golf course. We can lay out a plan while swinging our clubs.

"Okay, but we will need written reports ASAP. Myself, done!"

***

We decided to hit the golf course at the old Norton Air Force Base. It used to be an officers-only private club, but it was now open to the public. The location was perfect as it was across from the Santa Ana River, where Anthony grew up... and Chris went missing. Sometimes it's good to get out of our offices and clear our heads as you determine a game plan.

"Anthony."

"Hey, Dean, good choice to get a round in while we work."

Liter was a scratch golfer, and I had about an 18 handicap, and that was being generous.

As I hacked around the golf course, Liter gave me the rundown of the evidence we had. Basically, it was a circumstantial evidence case considering time, location, contacts with Chris on that day, and the wiretap that pushed it close to the filing line. After shooting an 89 and Liter firing a 73, we sat down for a cold beer and finished up our game plan.

As we put the puzzle together, we both realized we needed to *turn* Peter Ramirez, but that will almost be impossible. The *fighter pilot* came out in me, and I made the decision to pull Clyde Baker out of prison and charge him with the murder of Chris. We both realized this was going to be a tough case, but we truly believed Clyde murdered Chris and helped his brother Jessie.

Speaking of Jessie Baker, we hit a dead end. We did have some information that he joined the *Merchant Marines* in 1976, but after that, there is no trace of him. We would keep searching.

PART II
THE TRIAL

Chapter 14

The next morning, I received the reports as requested by the homicide team. I re-read them and found myself second-guessing myself. Did we have enough evidence to meet the criminal standard of proof beyond a reasonable doubt? I made the decision to file a murder complaint, knowing a case may get better or worse during the pre-trial and trial stages. And ethically, I truly believe Clyde was the *killer* or *co-killer* with his brother. Also, with the filing, it may trigger another phone call from Clyde Baker. This time from our local jail, as that is where he would be transferred after we filed the case.

As I drafted the complaint, it was the first time I put Christine Stone's name down on a formal legal document. It brought back so many memories and a combination of anger and sadness. But I had to set that aside as I had a job to do.

Liter came by and walked the complaint to the Court Clerk's Office. Once that is done, the clock starts. We have ten days to conduct a preliminary hearing, a hearing before a judge to determine whether we have enough evidence to proceed. There would be pre-trial motions and more. I was more than ready to start the battle, and it was going to be a battle.

After the filing, the press got wind of it, and the next morning, the headline read: "30 Plus Year Old Cold Case Solved." Well, they jumped the gun because we still had to prove it in a court of law. The good news was that the case was assigned to Judge Warren for all proceedings. As I said, she was tough but followed the rule of law.

The first court date was the arraignment the following morning. The team and I walked over to the courthouse the next day. The courthouse was located across from my office. We could access it through the back entryway. It was a beautiful, classic building built in 1927. It had a beautiful landscape, which included a fountain and a sundial plaque. The interior was split in half. There was a newer section built years later, but our case was scheduled on the original side in Court Room 1. The design of the courtroom featured classic columns and beautiful spaced windows with beautiful high ceilings. One feature I loved about the courtroom was the old seats in the public area. They were wood with *hat racks* built on the backside of the chairs, made for the days when men wore fedoras and the ladies wore their fancy headwear. The council table was beautiful. A huge cherrywood carved piece of art, and our chairs were an antique wood design with spindles on the back and roller wheels on the legs. It truly felt like church to this Catholic boy. As it should be, a place for justice to be served, especially for the families of lost loved ones.

I still get chills thinking about it. On the other hand, it wasn't a very safe courthouse, as the defendants would walk down the same stairways and hallways we did. Of course, they were escorted, but the Marshalls would have to clear the hallways.

As we walked into the courtroom, Clyde Baker was already sitting in the juror's box—where they would put defendants for arraignments in a red jumpsuit—high risk and shackled. I sat with the team, awaiting the judge to take the bench. Clyde was one of fifteen arraignments this morning.

While we were waiting, in walked Deputy Public Defender Vance Wright, a member of their murder team and one of their best attorneys. As he walked by, he said, "Good morning, Anthony. I see we will be going at it again."

"If you mean the case of Clyde Baker, yes, we will," I said.

As Vance went to talk to Clyde, my team looked at me and said, "Here we go again."

I told them it was always better to have a good defense attorney as it cuts down an appeal if we are successful, especially when it's the number one reason for appeals to be reversed—the incompetence of counsel. We all agreed it was for the best.

The judge approached the bench, and the bailiff said the standard, "All Rise, Judge Lisa Warren." We were hoping she would call our case first, and she did.

"In the People vs. Clyde Baker, how do you plead?"

"Not guilty."

"Attorney Wright, are you assigned to this case?"

"Yes, Your Honor."

"Does your client have the means to hire his own attorney?"

At that, Clyde said, "Does it look like it?"

Deputy Public Defender Wright told his client to hush as he proceeded to tell the judge he did not have the means to hire an attorney.

Judge Wright then noted, "Well, then, the Public Defender's Office will be assigned to defend you. There is no need to determine bail because... number one, he is in prison for another matter, and two, this is a first-degree murder charge, and that means no bail. Anything further?"

Public Defender Wright then asked if his client could be held at County Jail throughout the proceedings.

The judge looked at me and said, "Deputy D.A. Garcia, good to see you again. Any objection to that request?"

"No, Your Honor."

"Well, good. We can proceed to a pre-preliminary hearing and preliminary hearing with the dates on the board unless you want a continuance?"

Deputy Public Defender Wright noted he needed a continuance as this is a complicated and weak case.

"I ain't waving no time," big mouth Clyde said.

"So be it. We will see you in eight days," the judge said.

That was the good thing about having a *vertical* courtroom, meaning Judge Warren would handle this case from start to finish. As we left, we could see Vance arguing with his new client before Clyde was removed from the courtroom.

As we discussed the next steps in the hallway, out walked Clyde, with two Marshalls escorting him. The press was there with cameras ready. To everyone's surprise, he turned and looked at me, saying, "Anthony, you're a punk and always were one. Sorry about your little girlfriend." As he smiled, he was pushed by the Marshalls, telling him to move on and to keep his mouth shut.

I had to keep my cool as reporters then surrounded us for comments. Of course, we could make no comments while the case was pending trial or even during the trial, according to the Code of Prosecutorial Conduct and the media. That never stopped the defense, and they moved on to Public Defender Wright. With that, we left the courthouse. Once outside, I looked at Mike, and without me saying a word, he said, "I'm on it." Of course, we were okay with Clyde being in our local County Jail phones!

***

The next morning, I woke up to read on the top of the fold, front page:

Suspected killer Clyde Baker smiles at Deputy District Attorney Garcia as he calls him a punk and mentions the victim was his girlfriend.

The news was accompanied by a full-blown picture.

Clyde actually looked like the *Joker* from the current Batman movies. One scary guy, I thought. In the body of the story, it went on to talk about the cold case and the young girl, Christine Stone, who went missing in 1969. They went on to say that Anthony Garcia and the suspect himself went to school with her, and attempts to contact her parents for the story were unsuccessful. They also went on to say Clyde was a member of the Loco's Motorcycle Gang and had a violent history. As I turned the page, there was a picture of Christine taken from our Sixth-Grade class photo, smiling with her fuzzy hair down to her shoulders. I cut it out, took it to the office, and pinned it to my corkboard to remind me why I do this job as well as to let Chris know she was never forgotten. I went to church that morning as I got strength from just being there and saying the prayers Grandma Garcia taught me.

It was a matter of less than twenty-four hours before Clyde made a phone call from the jail to his daughter, Debbie Baker. I headed over to the sheriff's office to listen in on the recording Mike had for us:

"Will you accept a collect call from Clyde Baker?"

"If I have to, yes."

"Debbie, what the hell did you tell those asshole detectives? They have me charged with murder, and my attorney said after reading the reports so far, you gave some damaging statements. Not only about the damn bike, but comments I made about what she deserved!"

"Well, I was scared, and they pressured me. The one detective, Sandy, was really nice, and she said they were just trying to figure out what happened to that poor girl."

"Well, from here on out, you won't talk to those cops, and if you do and I get out, I will make sure you and those kids are out of my mobile home!"

"Dad, did you kill her?"

With that, the phone went dead as Clyde hung up on Debbie.

"It sure is a good thing that some crooks are stupid and hotheaded," Liter said, and we all agreed.

"There's one more disturbing call. This one to Peter Ramirez," Mike said.

"How many calls do they get?" I asked.

We later found out Clyde was lying and had said he was calling his attorney.

Peter accepted the collect call immediately.

"I read the paper. What the hell, homie? How are you holding up?"

"They have some shit on me, but my lawyer thinks it is a weak case. I need you to pay Debbie a visit and tell her to keep her mouth shut. I also want you to give a message to that punk Anthony's family who still lives in Okieville."

"That's kind of dangerous. He is the prosecutor."

"Just tell them to back off. You know how we do."

"I'll see what we can do."

We all looked at each other, and it was time to visit Peter Ramirez as soon as possible. I would have to stay out of this interview, and the detectives headed out to his place with a determined look on their faces. Liter had that scowl, and this is when I appreciated his toughness. They were trying to intimidate our witnesses and me as the prosecutor. Good luck with that! Fighting instincts kicked in.

As our team was heading out to visit our witness and Peter Ramirez, I received a phone call from Deputy Public Defender Vance Wright.

"Vance, how can I help you?"

"Well, Anthony, seems like a pretty weak case to me, and you can't even say for sure the recovered skeletal remains are those of your victim."

"Well, Vance, you know me, I would not have filed this case if I didn't believe he was guilty." The best part of this conversation came next. "Oh, and by the way, I have some more discoveries for you. Your client sure likes to talk on the phone."

"What!? I told him to keep his mouth shut. That's a confidential conversation."

"Not when it's between him and non-law enforcement. I'll send you the tapes after we get off the phone. Enjoy them."

"The press is driving me crazy. We are going to waive a preliminary hearing as we both know all you have to do is put the detective on the stand, and he can testify using hearsay."

We both knew this was allowed in the State of California. I then asked, "No plea offer, Vance?"

"My client says hell no, and he won't waive time. He wants his trial now."

As we hung up the phone, I knew we had some long days ahead of us to get ready for the trial. I knew Vance did not like his client rushing him as most defense attorneys like to *age* their cases in an attempt to have our witnesses forget certain details or, even better for them, witnesses being unavailable after several years. However, you can't get older than a 30-year-old cold case, and we would be ready to go.

It was time to contact the victim's family regarding the trial dates. Mrs. Stone, along with brothers Johnny and Bobby, had to be notified. But first, I waited to hear what our detectives had to say about the threats to our witnesses and my family members.

Chapter 15

We made the decision to break up the team for the threat assessment contacts. Mike and I would pay Peter a visit, and we would send Sandy to talk to Debbie Baker and Zona.

As Mike and I arrived at the gang headquarters, we saw that their bikes were all lined up.

"Must be a staff meeting," I said to Mike. "Well, let's interrupt what's ever so important."

As we approached the door, we could hear Peter discussing what may be a plan to contact our witnesses. I wanted to kick the door in, but I thought better of it as we did not have a warrant. So, we knocked on the door. Peter answered after several knocks.

"What now? I'm kind of busy, Detective Liter."

"Can we come in for a minute?"

Peter stepped out the door and said, "Whatever you want to talk to me about, we can do it right here."

"Look, Mr. President, we got word that you were planning some witness intimidation regarding our case against your boy, Clyde. You know, that's a felony, and we would love nothing better to do but get you and your crew off the streets," I said.

"Well, it sounds like you're intimidating a witness, boys," Peter answered.

"Oh, you have no idea what intimidating a witness is," I responded, "and you don't want to find out."

"Well, I don't know what you're talking about, but I look forward to seeing you during the trial."

"Oh, you will see us, alright," Mike reached into his back pocket and pulled out a subpoena ordering Mr. Peter Ramirez to be in Superior Court on the day the trial was to begin. "Here, you have been served. Have a nice day."

On that note, we left.

***

I arrived at Debbie Baker's mobile home and knocked on the door.

A few seconds later Debbie answered the door.

"Detective Sandy Smith," I reintroduced myself with my badge.

"I remember you. You're the nice one. Come in, don't mind the mess, but it is tough being a single parent." She cleared a spot on her orange-colored couch and said, "Here, have a seat."

As I sat down, I noticed the family pictures on the wall. Debbie was with her children in one photo and appeared to be with Clyde when she was a young girl in another.

As I looked at them, Debbie said, "You're here to talk about my father again, right?"

I told Debbie we had Clyde's trial scheduled in the near future, and she was considered a witness.

"I knew, at some point, I would be called upon as a witness, but I have to tell you, I'm scared." Debbie then began to tell me about her upbringing. "My father was a mean person, and as a kid, I was always afraid of him and his buddies."

"You mean his fellow gang members?"

"Yes. I mean, he never physically assaulted me, but I saw how he treated my mother. He would come home drunk, and if he didn't like something my mom did, he would yell at her and, at times, beat her. Now, when he assaulted her, he never did it in front of me. I would hide in my room and could hear it. At times, I would run outside and hide in the fields until it was dark and come home. The next morning, on one occasion, I saw my mother with a black eye. I knew then he would hit her. But they would always make up with a ride to Laughlin or Vegas. My mom loved to gamble. It was on one of those trips that she lost her life in a shootout with a rival gang. So, yes, I'm scared."

"Well, Debbie, you have every right to be. Has your dad been in contact with you since we last spoke?" I asked, knowing that he had.

Debbie looked up at his picture, then back to me. "Yes, he called me from jail and told me I was the reason he was being charged with murder and told me to keep my mouth shut."

I told Debbie she was a very important witness and shared with her the phone conversations we overheard. This would probably stop all conversations with her dad, but I had no choice as we didn't want any harm coming to her from the motorcycle gang, specifically Peter Ramirez.

Sometimes, one can come to trust a homicide detective, and I felt Debbie felt that way with me.

"We are going to have a jury trial soon, and we want to make sure you're okay. Of course, you can't tell us what happened the summer Christine went missing, but you can sure help us with facts that occurred years later."

Debbie shook her head and said, I understand."

I then asked Debbie, "Why did you ask your dad if he killed her?"

"I'm not sure, it's the way he becomes angry about it, and I keep thinking about the bike he gave me. It was hers, wasn't it? That poor girl was probably around my age when he gave the bike to me. I just wanted to know if it was him who killed Christine."

"Well, you have my card, and if you need anything, call, especially if Peter or his boys come to visit."

"Oh, I'm not afraid of Peter. He's an old softie at heart. I call him Uncle Pete."

"Okay, well, thank you for your time, and we will see you in court, if not before."

***

Mike and I then paid a visit to Tony's cousin, Zona. Sandy was able to join us as Zona's house was across the street, five houses down from the trailer park where Debbie Baker lived on San Bernardino Avenue.

Zona was sitting out on her front lawn with several of her cousins, who would be Tony's cousins as well. She welcomed us with open arms and pulled out a few folding chairs for us to sit on. It was quite nice as there was a nice breeze, and she had two beautiful elm trees out front. She offered us a glass of lemonade, which we gladly accepted. She introduced us to her family, one whose name was Roberta. A kind of a smartass who said, "It's about time you guys solved the case of our friend, Christine."

Zona hushed Roberta and asked, "How can I help you, Detective Liter?"

We proceeded to tell her about the possible threats and that the trial dates had been set.

"I know the so-called biker gang, and I'm fine. At my age, the only person I fear is the Lord." Zona was very religious and was a dedicated member of the St. Joseph Catholic Church in Loma Linda.

Roberta piped in and said, "I know those *old farts*. They are all a bunch of losers. Plus, Cousin Michael just got out of the Navy, and he is living with his mom in the corner house. He's built like a *ship* and has good artillery."

"Well, there shouldn't be a need for that, but we just wanted to make you aware," I said.

With that, we parted ways, and on our way out, we looked at each other and said now we know why Tony is so tough. However, we would keep an eye on his family.

When we got back to the office, we called the Police Chief of the City of Redlands, where Tony lived. We gave the chief all the details, and he said it wouldn't be an issue for patrol to cruise by Tony's house when they were on duty. Tony and the Police Chief, John Brown, had actually attended high school together.

It was now time to prepare for the trial!

Chapter 16

Fridays are pre-trial and motion days. As we entered Judge Warren's courtroom, I felt like I had two popsicles in my pockets, ready to melt if we had to prolong hearings. I had briefed the court on the admissibility of the phone conversations, and we had briefed the court on possible witness tampering, as well as the subtle threat to me in the hallway after our last hearing.

Clyde was sitting at the counsel table with his attorney, Vance Wright. As Judge Warren entered, we stood, but Clyde refused to stand and sat in his place, looking straight at me with a scowl on his face.

"Counsel, please have a seat. I have read and considered your pre-trial briefs. I am ready to rule. Any arguments on either side?"

"No, Your Honor, the people submit."

"Mr. Wright?"

"Well, Your Honor, as I indicated in my brief, I believe it was a violation of Mr. Baker's Miranda Rights, and if not, at least his attorney-client privilege."

"Mr. Wright, I read your brief. Your client was not being interviewed by law enforcement at the time and made his phone calls of his own free will. As to attorney-client privilege, he was not talking to you or any of your investigators. He, in fact, waived any privileges he had by discussing the case with both Mr. Ramirez and Ms. Baker. So, your motion to exclude the conversations is denied. Next, if I hear of any witness threats, I will allow the prosecution to draft a jury instruction indicating as much."

"That's *B.S.,* and you know it, Anthony."

"Mr. Wright, you will control your client."

At that, Vance told Clyde to shut up.

"I note you haven't waived time, so we will begin jury selection in two weeks. Anything further?"

"No, Your Honor," I replied.

"None here, Your Honor," Vance said.

As we left the courthouse, we saw Peter sitting in the courtroom. We asked what he was doing there.

"I was just making sure the trial was still scheduled as I was told."

Liter jumped in. "Peter, don't be stupid. You heard the judge. Any witness intimidation and it will not only help our case, but I will be able to put these handcuffs on you. Try me!"

At the office, our trial strategy was discussed. It wouldn't be a long trial as we did not have many witnesses, but like all trials, jury selection would be extremely important.

We discussed the witness list and order.

"We would fly out Mrs. Stone and her two sons. They would, of course, need to take the stand to lay the foundation regarding their missing daughter and sister from years ago. The brothers may also give us a good foundation regarding the Baker boys. Along with the forensic anthropologist, we will put Zona, Debbie Baker, and Peter Ramirez on the stand. Along with you, detectives, regarding the discovery of Christine's remains and other foundational matters. Of course, what's missing is Jessie Baker. Last we knew, he was a Merchant Marine. It would be like finding a needle in a haystack."

We knew it was possible that Jessie's brother Clyde may use him as his defense. It's called *Third-Party Culpability,* which means blaming someone else. In this case, his brother.

Liter then spoke up. "That flower sticker that Zona got in her mailbox was sent to the lab as there was no return address on the envelope. Both the flower sticker was checked for fingerprints and the envelope for DNA, and both came back negative. We believe it was a form of threat from Clyde and his boys, but we could not prove it. This would be a totally circumstantial evidence trial, but I truly feel Clyde alone or Clyde and his brother murdered Christine Stone."

Chapter 17

The morning of the trial, I did my ritual 4:00 AM run before the wife and kids woke up. It helped me stay calm during trial days. I would then have my coffee and a light breakfast, usually a bagel, as I read the morning paper. The headline that morning was:

"30+ Year Old Cold Case to Start Today"

In the body of the report, it quoted elected District Attorney Greg Matthews, my boss, saying we have a very strong case and justice will be done. Really? This was coming from a District Attorney that had never tried a murder case. He was a politician that loved a headline. Thanks a lot, boss, is what came to mind.

The family was now up, and I got to kiss and hug the kids goodbye and get the good luck hug from Rachel as I headed out the door.

The plan was to meet the team early that morning. Mrs. Stone and her sons were staying at the Ramada Inn down the street as they had gotten in the day before. I would meet with them after our first day of jury selection. The detectives were there bright and early. I had Mike and Sandy do some follow-up to make sure the witnesses would be in court, and Liter would be my

Investigating Officer, meaning he would be sitting with me throughout the trial.

As we entered the courtroom, I noticed several reporters milling around in the hallway. Defendant Clyde Baker was sitting with his attorney. He had him dressed in a suit, of course. The temperature in the courtroom was warm as you could never cool off this historical part of the courthouse in the middle of California summers. We were handed a list of potential jurors, and as I was scanning them, Vance said he had a motion to submit prior to the jury panel coming in.

"Well, that's new to me. It would have been nice to have been given notice," I said.

"Relax, Anthony. It won't take long."

We both approached the bailiff and asked if we could see the judge before the panel was brought in. The bailiff granted us permission, and we entered Judge Warren's chambers.

"What now, gentlemen?"

"Well, we want a motion in limine," Vance said.

A motion in limine is a request outside the presence of the jury to exclude certain testimony.

"What, now?" I asked.

"We don't want any mention of my client's membership in the motorcycle gang. We are talking about what happened years ago when my client was a kid."

What we discovered was that the Baker brothers were actually two years behind in school, making them 15 years old at the time Christine went missing. And that made sense as these two bullies were physically built like mini bodybuilders.

Judge Warren turned to me.

"Your Honor, we agree that Clyde's gang membership has no relevance in a thirty-year-old case. However, as indicated by yourself, if there were any threats to witnesses, there could be a jury instruction as such. Also, if Mr. Baker should take the stand, we intend to diminish his credibility with his prior record, including the crimes he committed in furtherance of his gang ties."

"Well, at this time, there will be no mention of any gang affiliation, and we will take up the other issues should he take the stand at that time. Are we clear?"

"Yes, Your Honor."

When we sat back down at the counsel table, I said to Liter, "No big deal regarding the gang affiliation. However, we both knew before the trial was over, it would come out somehow. In fact, the newspaper has already talked about his membership in the gang. I'm sure we will both be asking the prospective jurors how much news media they have been reading or watching regarding this case."

With that, the jury panel was brought in. I did recognize a couple of jurors, but other than that, it looked like a good panel. The remainder of the day was spent attempting to get the best jury possible to hear our case. We were looking for an educated panel that would understand the complexity of a circumstantial evidence case and one that would be fair and ethical as they determined their verdict.

The courtroom had seemed extra warm that day. The old ceiling fans did nothing but blow the hot air around. We, in fact, lost one juror to heat exhaustion. However, by the end of the day, we had twelve jurors seated with two alternates in place. It was a long day, but we felt good about our jury. It was Thursday, and opening statements would not start until Monday as the courts did not conduct jury trials on Fridays. This gave us the weekend for final preparation. You see, when you're in trial, you don't get weekends off if you want to be successful.

After court, I decided to stop by and see my dad on the way home. He lived in the community of East Highland. He was always good about bouncing off trial strategies, as he had seen a lot in life, and I loved his wisdom.

I could hear him playing his guitar to the tune of "Kansas City Here I Come" when I entered the door. He lived alone in a newer two-story home. His second wife, my stepmom, had died of cancer two years prior.

As I walked in, my dad said, "Hey, what's up, boy?" He called me boy or Anthony, depending on the seriousness of the conversation.

As I looked upon his staircase, I saw a string of empty beer cans across the middle of the stairway. I said, "What's up with that, Pop?"

"Well, Anthony, I got a phone call the other day, and when I answered it, the caller said, 'You better back off. We know where you live, Tony.' I said in response, 'What are you waiting for? Come get me.'"

You see, my dad had the same name, Anthony Garcia, and kept his phone number and address in the phone book. I asked him many times to take his number and address out of the phone book, and he always refused, saying, "No one intimidates me." The Marine always came out in him at these moments. He had his shotgun ready and his 9mm handgun at his side.

"Pop, this case I'm trying is stirring up some anger. They think I live here.

"Well, son, that's good, as they can't find you."

How I loved this man, but he would frustrate me as well.

"Pop, did they say who they were?"

"No."

That would make it tough to prove in court that it was coming from Clyde and his punk gang members. Well, we both agreed at least that I would let the Sheriff's Department know. We went on to talk about the family and how he was doing. He lived his life in the moment, saying, "Every day is like extra icing on the cake—enjoy it while you're here."

My first call as I left my dad's house was to Liter.

"What?! We will have patrol run by his house during our shifts."

I was fortunate that Dean Liter lived in East Highland, and I knew he would check on Pop as well, both being former Marines. It was a true brotherhood. Once a U.S. Marine, always one!

With Pop taken care of, it was now time to prepare for opening statements. I knew the weekend would be spent outlining my presentation and selecting the photographs we would use in presenting our evidence.

Chapter 18

After my morning routine, I headed to the office, focused and ready for the trial. I met Liter, and we headed to the courthouse, where we would proceed with opening statements. We had met with Mrs. Stone and her sons the prior week, and they were ready to testify but were very anxious.

As we entered the courtroom, we saw several gang members wearing their colors and trying to get into the courtroom. It was a good thing they had the jurors sitting in the deliberation room as they did not see the argument between the gang members and the Marshalls about wearing their *colors* jackets with a red skeleton head on the back. Peter Ramirez was with them, and he had no idea he would not be able to be in the courtroom as he was a witness.

As we sat at the counsel table, we realized it was going to be another warm day, but the pitchers of water were full, and the overhead fans were actually working. Of course, it was ten in the morning. The courtroom was full, and the skulls were seated with their colors on. Like I told Liter, it would come out eventually that Clyde was a gang member.

Judge Warren entered the courtroom, and we all rose per the bailiff's order. As we then sat down, Judge Warren asked if there was anything further before the jury was brought in. We requested the standard motion to exclude witnesses, and the judge agreed, saying, "Anyone a witness in this matter is excluded from the courtroom until you are called to the witness stand."

Mrs. Stone and her sons knew this was coming, and it was no problem. However, Peter Ramirez stood up and said, "This is not right."

Judge Warren then had the bailiff escort Peter out. The tone was set, it was going to be a battle, but we were ready.

"Counsel, are we ready to proceed."

"Yes, Your Honor."

As the jury was escorted into the courtroom, it was the custom to stand until they were seated. At least, it was still my custom as these were citizens that took time away from their busy lives to serve the public.

Opening Statement

Like a good book, it is always best to start your opening statement to the jury with a passion that will grab their attention, like the book you can't put down once you read the first chapter.

"Mr. Garcia, you may proceed with the *people's* opening statement."

"Thank you, Your Honor." As I stood, I had a habit of checking my tie as I couldn't stand newscasters or others whose ties were crooked at the neck. I know I'm weird that way. I also kept telling myself to keep my personal emotions in check as I had a job to do. The courtroom was really warming up, and of course, I thought of those darn popsicles again, but in a good way.

"Ladies and gentlemen of the jury, I want to first thank you for your service. What you're about to hear is a summary of the witnesses and evidence that will be presented. Consider this a jigsaw puzzle, with every single piece as important as the others. This is a case about a vibrant, loving young girl, Christine Stone, who went missing in the summer of 1970. Yes, over thirty years ago, what we call a cold case, but what is never cold to the loved one's family."

I had to choke back a tear and proceed.

"You will hear from her mother that the family moved to a part of the county we call Okieville from Oklahoma during the Great Depression. It was a wonderful place to grow up. A rural community surrounded by fields of wheat, with giant sprinkler systems on big silver wheels, silos, and beautiful orange groves

117

as the backdrop. A wonderful elementary school, Victoria Elementary, and families from all different backgrounds and cultures. This is where I met Christine, a classmate, and dear friend. It was the summer after our last year, 6th grade, at our elementary school that she went missing. You will hear testimony that they thought she was your typical runaway teen, like so many across our nation, who have their pictures posted on milk cartons, but early this year, all that changed. The day was January 2, 2003. Construction workers were moving ground, preparing for more *tilt-up* buildings… just what we need, right? When they started to grade the dirt, human skeletal remains were found. Found in a location where two huge silos once stood on Victoria Avenue. A place where we all played as kids. At this time, the San Bernardino County Sheriff's Homicide Team responded, with Detective Dean Liter taking the lead. He is sitting in court today with me as he is my lead investigator."

With that, I had Liter stand up.

"You will hear from her mother and brothers about the day Christine went missing. You will also hear from a dear friend of hers, Zona Montes, who last saw her. You will then hear from Forensic Anthropologist Dr. Stephen Anderson. Dr. Anderson will outline his findings regarding the skeletal remains we believe are those of Christine Stone. He will say that it is the remains of a

118

person between the ages of 10 years to 16 years and most like that of a female."

"OBJECTION! Your Honor, I don't believe that is the case."

"Mr. Wright, you will have the right to cross-examine all witnesses. Your objection is noted but overruled. You may proceed, Mr. Garcia," Judge Warren said.

"Thank you, Your Honor. I will let the expert explain what he found. You will hear from the defendant's daughter, Debbie Baker, regarding a purple Schwinn stingray bicycle that her father had given her from his childhood days. As well as phone conversations regarding the disappearance of Christine.

We will call Peter Ramirez to the stand, and he will tell you about the day Christine went missing. He was close friends with both the defendant and his brother, Jessie Baker. Speaking of Jessie Baker, you will hear that since he and his brother were abandoned, no one has seen or heard from him. And finally, you will hear from Detective Mike Jones, who has listened to conversations between the defendant and both his daughter and Peter Ramirez, evidence obtained by a legal wiretap.

We ask you to pay close attention to each piece of evidence and the witness testimony before you determine whether the defendant is guilty or not. However, we do believe when the puzzle pieces are put together, you will find the defendant GUILTY of the murder of Ms. Christine Stone, a young girl who lost her life way too young. Thank you."

As I sat down, I took a deep breath. It was like the first series of a football game. You're anxious and stressed and ready to go, but until you're in the game, that energy builds up in you like an old orange crush soda on a hot summer day.

Liter leaned over and said, "Good job, Tony. You had all the jurors' attention, with some shaking their heads in disbelief."

"Are you ready to give your opening statement, Mr. Wright?" Judge Warren asked.

"Your Honor, we will wait until we start our defense."

You see, the defense does not have to give an opening statement at the start of the trial, or at all for that matter. The *people* have the burden of proof, and that's how it should be.

"Mr. Garcia, are the people ready to proceed?"

"Yes, Your Honor, we would like to call our first witness, Mrs. Helen Stone."

As Mrs. Stone entered the courtroom, you could hear a pin drop. She was escorted in by one of our victim advocates. They were such a tremendous help to our office in helping victims through the judicial process, especially the trial phase.

As Mrs. Stone stood on the witness stand, the court clerk gave her the standard admonishment. "Mrs. Stone, please state your name for the record."

"Helen Stone."

"Please raise your right hand. Do you swear to tell the truth and nothing but the truth, so help you God?"

"I do."

"Mr. Garcia, you may proceed."

"Mrs. Stone, tell me how you're related to Christine."

"She is my daughter."

"Can you share with us who she was?"

"My daughter was my firstborn. She was full of energy from the day she was born. She loved to be outdoors, and boy, could she run. When she got into elementary school, she loved to race the boys and, as you know, loved all sports."

"How would I know Mrs. Stone?"

"Well, you went to school with her, and she always talked about you. Sometimes it was good and sometimes not so good,"

Mrs. Stone smiled. "She would come home and talk about how fun school was, and she had many friends. She loved life."

"Tell me about her home life."

"OBJECTION! What does this have to do with anything?"

"It's foundational, Mr. Wright," Judge Warren said. "Mrs. Stone, you may proceed."

"Well, we were close, I mean her brothers and me. Her father was an alcoholic who was verbally abusive and sometimes physical with me, but he never touched Christine. He truly loved her. I recall the Christmas he surprised her with a new purple bike."

"Can you describe that bicycle?" I asked.

"Sure, she was so excited, it was a *stingray* with those long seats, and she loved riding it."

"What happened to her bicycle?"

"It was taken, and her father was very upset about it. He made her go look for it. He went out looking in his truck as well but ended up in Joe's bar, like he always did at the end of the day, getting home late. But worse than that, it was the last time I saw my daughter." With that, Mrs. Stone began to cry.

"Do you need a break, Helen?" I asked.

"No, I can keep going. It's just really hard."

"Okay, can you tell us what she was wearing the last time you saw her?"

"Yes, a blouse. I'm not sure of the color, jeans, and her favorite shoes, P.F. Flyers."

"Can you tell us about an item back then called *flower power* stickers?"

"Yes, she loved them. She placed one on her bike and had them all over her room."

"Did she have them with her when she went missing?"

"I can't say for sure, but I wouldn't be surprised. They were like her signature on life. She loved the name *flower power*. That's how she saw herself."

"When she went missing, what happened then?"

"She hadn't come home by nightfall, and that was not our rule. In fact, all the kids in the neighborhood had that rule. There were no real streetlights, and except for the glow of Norton Air Force Base, it would get pretty dark. I loaded up her brothers in the car, and we drove around the neighborhood looking for her. We stopped by the local stores, including the new Circle K, which was her favorite, and no one had seen her since earlier that afternoon. We then went back home, and her dad's truck was in the driveway. He had been drinking again and blew it off, saying, 'She probably ran away.' I was not happy with his attitude, so I called the Sheriff's Department."

"What happened then?"

"A very nice Deputy Sheriff came to our home and took all the information we had, including what her brothers had to say about the Baker boys and a friend of theirs by the name of Peter. He asked if there was any reason she may have run away. As I looked at my husband, I said *no,* and to this day, I wish I had told the truth. I know she was very upset about how I was mistreated by my now-deceased husband and how he treated her brothers. Maybe they would have looked harder for her. The next morning, I called my PTA friends, and they were so supportive. They helped me make some *missing* flyers with Christine's photo and a contact number. We then placed them all over the neighborhood."

"Why did you move two weeks after she went missing?"

"My husband said she ran away, and if she ran anywhere, it would be back to Oklahoma. It gave me hope, so we moved. As you know, we never found her and have prayed for years that she did run away and was still alive, living a better life than I could give her."

Mrs. Stone began to break down.

"No further questions, Your Honor. But we request a break before Mrs. Stone is cross-examined."

"Granted," Judge Warren replied.

During the break, we made sure Mrs. Stone was okay.

"You did really well, and as we discussed, the defense attorney now has a chance to ask you questions."

"Mr. Wright, do you have any questions?" Judge Warren asked.

"Yes, just a few, Your Honor."

"Mrs. Stone, why did you leave your home and move out of the state?"

"As I said, my husband truly felt she ran away. There was no reason not to believe that. He also talked me into believing that she may have run back to Oklahoma, where she had family. I prayed he was right."

"Did he ever physically abuse your daughter?"

"No, he assaulted me on occasion and punished my boys but never Christine. He was an alcoholic and eventually died of liver disease, but he loved Christine as he went into a deep depression when she went missing."

"I have nothing further, Your Honor."

"Anything further, Mr. Garcia?

"No, Your Honor."

"You may step down, Mrs. Stone," Judge Warren instructed. "Your next witness, Mr. Garcia?"

"That would be Johnny Stone."

Johnny was brought to the witness stand and was sworn in. He testified that he was Christine's brother.

Johnny stated, "I recall the last day I saw my sister. She was upset as the Baker boys had taken her bike."

"Do you see one of them in the court today?" I asked.

"Yes," Johnny pointed to Clyde sitting at the table.

"Let the record reflect he has identified the defendant," I said.

"My dad was home, and he was very upset, as always, as Christine said her bike was stolen at the Circle K, and my dad made her go out to find it. We went with her, and that's when she told us she was assaulted by the Baker brothers, and they took her bike."

"OBJECTION! Your Honor, hearsay."

"It will be allowed in as foundational only. You may proceed," Judge Warren overruled the objection.

"Well, we didn't look anymore as we knew what happened. Our dad also went out looking but ended up at the bar. We then posted flyers on telephone poles and prayed Christine would come home. The Sheriff's Department thought it was possible she ran away. About a week later, we ran into the *bullies,* I mean Clyde and Jessie Baker, at Jim's Store, and they threatened us about the Sheriff's Deputies coming to talk to them. I truly feel they killed her!!"

"OBJECTION, Your Honor! That is speculation," shouted Public Defender Wright.

Judge Warren sustained the objection and said that the jurors should disregard that statement. Well, as we all know, that's hard to get out of one's mind.

"We have no further questions, Your Honor."

"Cross-examination, Mr. Wright?"

"No, Your Honor."

We then called Christine's other brother, Bobby Stone, to the stand, and he confirmed what his twin brother had testified to.

The day was almost over, and we were excused early. Overall, we felt good about our first witnesses, but I felt terrible about putting Christine's mom through that pain all over again.

Chapter 19

It was the summer of 1968, and I was promoted at my job at Norton Air Force Base. We all anticipated the C-5A Galaxy Military Transport plane. It was a sight to see, and I took Christine and the boys to see it and marvel at its size. An Air Force pilot saw us and gave my kids a tour. Since that day, Christine told me she wanted to join the Air Force and travel around the world. She was so excited she went home and started to read everything she could about airplanes in the latest edition of encyclopedias I had purchased.

"Christine, I'm not sure how many women are in the Air Force, but it's a good career."

"Mom, I want to be a pilot! I'm as good as any boy. Just ask Anthony. I'm his wide receiver on his football team at school, and I'm as fast as any boy."

"Christine, I know that's true, but with time you might feel different, but I love that you have goals."

My little girl was growing up to be a true leader. She was a straight-A student and a good athlete. That Christmas, I wanted to get something special for the kids. Their dad had been gone for over a year now. We were struggling, but I saved enough money in an old coffee can to have a decent Christmas.

That summer, I did extra work at a local packing house. We were surrounded by orange groves, and we had a very vibrant agriculture economy selling oranges across the country. After work, I would bring home a box of succulent oranges that were so delicious on a hot summer day. When you bit into them, it was like biting into a creamsicle with juice dripping down the corner of your mouth. I loved that part-time job, and so did my kids. The summer flew by, making us realize that our little community of Okieville was the best place to raise kids.

Fall came, and then winter. I recall the Christmas tree that year. It was so tall we had to cut off the top just so it would fit in the living room. Christine, of course, took the top to make a little tree in her room. We had so much fun decorating the tree, and the kids loved the final step of throwing silver tinsel strands all over the tree. It could be a mess, but it was beautiful.

The next day, Christine asked if she could attend her friend Zona's cookie-making party. I said yes, just so she would take her brothers. That would give me a chance to wrap presents. It was a good time. At the Base *commissary* store, they were selling Schwinn bicycles. I took all the money I had saved and spent it on my kids. The boys were getting this new car set called *hot wheels* with orange tracks. They would love them.

Christine had earned a new bike. She loved the bikes the boys were riding, of course. And she loved the color purple. I pulled out my purse and was twenty dollars short as I looked at the perfect bike for her. I lowered my head to say a prayer and heard my name called.

"Mrs. Stone?"

"Yes."

It was Mr. Garcia, Christine's good friend, Anthony's dad. He worked at the Base as well and was a very handsome man. Everyone liked him, and now I know why. He asked about the kids, and I told him my story.

"Well, I have an idea. I'm getting my boys the same bike. Let's see if they'll give me a deal if we purchase three instead of one."

Lo and behold, it worked. They knocked off thirty dollars, and it was done. But Mr. Garcia also insisted I keep the extra ten dollars. As a gift to me for being so nice to his boys as a PTA member. He was truly a saint. I hugged him and thanked him! As he walked away, he turned and said, "Just don't sell Anthony Jr. any more popsicles. Merry Christmas."

I will always remember this kind man.

It was one of the best Christmases in our lives. I was able to give my children some gifts, but the best gift of all was the love we shared.

Christine hugged me and said, "Mom, you are the best."

"Don't say that too loud. Your brothers still believe in Santa," I said.

Christine called her bike a *jet* and jumped on it, taking off on our typical warm Southern California Christmas day. She was the happiest I had ever seen her.

But today, as I got back from court, I couldn't stop crying. Thank God Johnny and Bobbie were with me. Why did they take my little girl from me? Why??!!

Chapter 20

After the first day of the trial, I headed home to do my most important job. I coached both of my kids in soccer. I was in charge of picking them up from my Aunt Tense's house, Zona's mom, then raced home to get ready for practice. Their mom worked in Brea, so it was a long day for her. I loved watching my son and daughter play sports. Watching my daughter, Christine Michele, run took me back to the days of Christine running past routes. We then got home, and I made my weekly cut-up hot dog and bean and cheese burritos. They were pretty darn good. Once I got the kids started on their homework, I started on mine for the next court day. The deal was that Rachel would get them cleaned up and ready for bed when she got home. It was great teamwork.

The night closed fast, and I ended it with my Jack and Coke and looked forward to another day in battle. However, when in a trial, things don't always go as planned. I got a call around midnight from Liter.

"Tony, we have information that Jessie Baker may be in Mexico. I'm sending the team to see if we can find him."

"Where in Mexico?" I asked.

"Not far. Baja, California. They are off and running as we

speak."

I thanked Liter and said I'll see him in the morning. It was almost impossible to get back to sleep. I was thinking about the case and also about the times, years ago, when my dad would take us to the Rosarito Beach Hotel every summer. I finally fell asleep with fish tacos floating in my head.

The next morning, we started the trial late, but that gave us some time to go over the facts with my next witness, Forensic Anthropologist Dr. Anderson. He was a tall, imposing man and, as I indicated, had a voice like *Lurch,* but he sure was smart.

We entered the courtroom on another hot day. Dr. Anderson took the stand and testified about his findings. He was a good witness, looking at the jurors when discussing his results. He told them that the skeletal remains were of someone Christine's age. He continued by mentioning the smoothness of the bones, which might be indicative of a female, and informing the jury of the clothing that had been found. It did help that *Levi's* jeans lasted forever, and the P.F. Flyers were still somewhat intact, but that could have been worn by a male just as well, or even more so. What did help was the *flower power* sticker found in the pocket of the jeans. I hoped that was enough for the jury. Dr. Anderson testified his final conclusion was that it was likely a female bone structure but could not say for certain.

"So you can't tell us for sure that the remains are of Christine Stone, can you?" Vance asked.

"No, sir. I can't," Dr. Anderson replied.

"No further questions, Your Honor."

As I indicated, we started late today, and we were well into the afternoon. Judge Warren had other matters to hear and excused us until the following day. That's how trials went. You had to be flexible.

The next morning, we were going to call Mike to the stand so he could talk about the wiretaps, but he was now in Mexico. Thus, we had to change our game plan. Next up, Peter Ramirez. Liter made sure Peter was in court in the morning.

As we walked into the courthouse, we saw a metal detector had been placed in the hallway leading to the courtrooms. We asked what was going on, and we were told it was a precaution as the Loco's Motorcycle Gang was going to be present. It made me feel better, but I was sure defense counsel Mr. Wright would not be happy.

"Your Honor."

"Yes, Mr. Wright?"

"What is going on? This is highly prejudicial to my client!"

"Well, Mr. Wright, the safety of our courtrooms outweighs any prejudicial issues you believe impact your case. I will note for the record that everyone entering this courtroom has to walk through the metal detector, including Deputy DA Garcia and Detective Liter. Your objection is noted for the record, but the detector stays for the rest of the trial."

As I turned back to look at the audience in the courtroom, I saw that the gang members were not allowed to wear their *colors* jackets, but they all had t-shirts on with *Loco's* and red skulls printed on the front. It's times like these that I really appreciate the First Amendment, Free Speech.

I poked Liter, and he whispered, "Fools."

"Yep," I said in response.

The jurors were brought in, and as they were seated, I saw a few of them giving the defendant, Clyde Baker, a look of disgust, or maybe they were looking at Vance. HA!

"Your Honor, at this time, we would like to call Mr. Peter Ramirez to the stand."

Well, talk about dirty looks... Peter sure gave me one as he walked to the stand.

After he was sworn in, I proceeded with the standard

foundational questions.

"How do you know the defendant?"

"Well, we grew up together. He's my homie."

"When was the last time you talked to him?"

"It's been years since, you know, he's been in prison."

"OBJECTION, Your Honor! May we approach the bench?"

"Yes, please approach."

"Mr. Wright?" Judge Warren inquired.

"I ask for a mistrial. The jurors had no idea Clyde was in prison, and now they do. This was highly unethical on behalf of the prosecution!"

"Mr. Garcia?"

"Well, I had no idea what his response would be. Also, the jurors will know Clyde has been in custody when we get to the *wiretap* evidence. We have had pre-trial motions regarding those phone conversations where the court agreed they would come into evidence."

"Motion for a mistrial is denied, but be very careful Mr. Garcia," Judge Warren said.

"I sure will, Your Honor."

137

"You may proceed, Mr. Garcia."

"Back in the summer of 1970, did you know Christine Stone?"

"Yes, I knew Chris, as we called her, and she was very much a tomboy, as I recall. She thought she was all that and a bag of chips. I thought she was your girlfriend," Peter testified with a smart smirk.

"When was the last time you saw her?"

"I don't remember. It was over thirty years ago."

"Did you see her the day she went missing?"

"I said I don't remember."

"Well, perhaps this will refresh your memory. Your Honor, I have transcripts of phone conversations between this witness and the defendant, Clyde Baker. I will lay the foundation at a later date with Detective Mike Jones. May I proceed?"

"Yes," Judge Warren said.

It was time to impeach this liar.

"Do you recall talking on the phone to the defendant prior to your being released from jail? Right after Detectives interviewed you?"

"Well, I'm not sure, maybe."

"Well, let's refresh your memory."

With that, we hit the play button on our laptop.

The jurors heard the first phone call from the jail to Clyde, where they discussed the detectives coming to see Peter, and Clyde shared with him that his daughter, Debbie, opened her big mouth. The jurors then heard Peter telling Clyde to hold onto his burner phone as he'll call him when he got out.

"Do you recall calling the defendant when you got out of jail?"

"Yes, I believe I did."

"What was the purpose of that call?"

"We are in business together, so I had some questions that I needed to ask."

"What kind of business, the business of covering up a murder?"

"OBJECTION!" Vance screamed.

"Counsel, approach the bench."

I knew I would get tongue-lashing at this time.

"Mr. Garcia, what are you doing?" Judge Warren inquired.

"I want a mistrial!" Vance said.

"Mr. Garcia?"

"Well, Your Honor, the remainder of the phone conversation will support my question, but I can rephrase it if you like."

"Okay, but you better be careful," Judge Warren warned. "Motion for a mistrial is denied. Ladies and gentlemen of the jury, please disregard the last question asked by Mr. Garcia. Mr. Garcia, you may proceed."

I knew, at that point, it was hard to erase statements in jurors' minds, plus the conversation said it all.

"Mr. Ramirez, what did you talk about?"

"I don't remember."

At that time, we played the taped conversation with the defendant on his burner phone. The jurors heard Peter question about the *cops* coming to see him in jail, and they had evidence that tied him to that missing girl. Clyde responded, "Don't sweat it." The conversation went on about Clyde and his brother assaulting Christine. The key point was as follows:

Peter: *Did you do her in?*

Clyde: *Well, let's just say my brother was the last to see her, but I may have helped a little. As I said before, she had it coming.*

The call ended with Peter's response, calling Clyde and his brother crazy and saying he would keep his mouth shut but that the heat was on.

After playing the recording, I indicated, "Your Honor, I have no further questions."

"Mr. Wright, cross-examination?"

"Yes, Your Honor, just one question," Vance said. "Mr. Ramirez you also said, 'No wonder your brother is out to sea somewhere.' Do you recall saying that?"

"I guess so. It's on the tape."

"Nothing further."

"May this witness be excused?" Judge Warren asked.

"Yes, Your Honor."

This ended another short day in trial. Overall, we felt it was a good day for the people. Now it was time to find out what, if anything, Mike and Sandy found out in Mexico.

Chapter 21

Mike and I checked into the Rosarito Beach Hotel in Baja, Mexico. According to the information we had, Jessie Baker was last seen in this area. It would be like finding a bagel in a Mexican bakery, but we had to give it a shot.

After a three-plus hour drive, we were hungry. The fish tacos were amazing at this little stand right at the entrance of the hotel. Corn tortilla, fresh fish, cabbage, and cilantro, with a tasty but hot salsa. Of course, we washed it down with a cold Corona.

After we ate, we checked into the old hotel, but it was beautiful, with paintings on the wall depicting the culture of Mexico. Our game plan after checking in was to take the one photo we had of Jessie Baker and hit the local bars and fishing ports. Mike liked the bar idea and said we needed to go undercover. That meant he wanted to drink beer. My room faced the ocean and was painted yellow and orange. I doubted I could sleep in this *pan dulce* but thought the ocean breeze and sound of the waves would help.

We met in the lobby, and Mike said the same thing about his room and reminded me not to drink the water unless I wanted to spend a lifetime on the toilet. He was good with words, but I got the point. We decided to start at *Papas and Beer* and go south towards Ensenada from there. No one at the hotel recognized Jessie's picture, and we doubted he stayed there.

Papas and Beer was hopping, they had a beach volleyball net set up, and folks were out playing at 9:00 AM. We stepped into the bar and ordered a Bloody Mary. Boy, was it spicey! We showed the bartender and waitresses the photo we had, and no one recognized Jessie. As the bartender said, "We have hundreds of *gringos* come in here with long hair and a beard like his." I told him he was a fisherman, and he directed us to several fishing docks. We stopped at several near the hotel. The smell was tough to handle, and like the smell of rotten fish, we lucked out at these stops. We were told the most likely place to find a fisherman was in Ensenada, but we were also advised to stop in *Puerto Nuevo* for lobster and to check their docks.

We sat down for lunch, and the young Mexican who told us to have lunch here was so right. We both ordered grilled lobster tails, homemade beans, rice, and fresh tortillas off the grill. Of course, we had a cold *Tecate* beer with this meal. We talked about the case and hoped the trial was going well. We hadn't talked to Liter in a couple of days, but we would contact him later today. Mike said he was in heaven. This is the best food in the world. He ordered an extra lobster tail and soaked it in butter. He had a glazed donut look on his face and said he was thinking of retiring here. He had already checked out some new condos that were built near the ocean across from the main highway next to a golf course. *Baja Del Mar,* I believe it was called. Well, who could blame him?

"Sandy, I haven't told anyone yet, but I put a down payment on one of those condos."

"Mike, you have earned it. I just hope you invite a friend over."

"Of course, I will."

After lunch, we walked towards the water. The ocean breeze had kicked up, and the mist against my face felt amazing. We approached the lobster boats and asked for the owner of the docks.

"Can we speak to *El Jefe,* the boss?" I asked.

"Si Siniora. He is right over there by the fishing nets."

We approached and introduced ourselves. We pulled out Jessie's picture, and he studied it for several seconds. Lucky for us, he spoke decent English.

"I can't say for sure if this is the same guy, but last I saw him, he was headed out to sea. That was about two weeks ago. I will

144

tell you this... he is not liked around here as he owes everyone money up and down the coast. My amigos tell me he was headed back to the States. That's all I know."

"Do you know if he had any friends or family here?"

"None. His friend was a beer, and his home... the bars. He's what you call a *loser* in your country. I hope we never see him again."

We thanked him and gave him our cards, telling him that in case Jessie returned, he should call us.

It was time to call Liter.

"Dean?"

"Yes, how did it go?"

"A dead end, so we are heading back, but the food and drinks were good," I said. "How's the trial going?"

"The trial is moving along, and it won't be long until the jury has it."

We shared with Liter the last contact we made in Puerto Nuevo, and he agreed it was time for us to get back.

Chapter 22

The Homicide Team was back, and I decided to put Liter on the stand to lay the foundation for the crime scene and Mike for the wiretap foundation. I would keep Sandy on standby, depending on how Debbie Baker did on the stand. It went as planned, and as we anticipated, Liter was hit on cross-examination regarding *Third-Party Culpability.*

"Detective Liter, after tagging the scene, you placed all items in evidence?"

"Yes, I did."

"I have no further questions."

"Cross-examination, Mr. Wright?"

"Yes, Your Honor."

"Detective Liter, do you know who Jessie Baker is?"

"Yes, I do."

"Did you ever consider him a suspect?"

"I did."

"But he is not here, right?"

"No, he's not."

"But if you have any idea where I can find him…"

"OBJECTION!" I said.

"Overruled," Judge Warren said. "Mr. Liter, please just answer the question."

"Okay, I don't know where he is."

"Isn't it possible you have the wrong brother?"

"Absolutely not. If anything, they are both responsible."

"I have nothing further, Your Honor."

We knew that was coming, so we let it go. There will be a jury instruction regarding Third-Party Culpability, and we should be fine. But score one for the defense on this day.

Liter went on to testify as follows:

"We cleaned up the crime scene with the crime lab and their processing staff. Again, we were fortunate that the construction workers came upon the skeletal remains, and we did all we could to find any further evidence at the oldest crime scene I had ever worked. After hours of sifting through dirt and rocks, I was confident I had gathered all the physical evidence we could. Including the *flower power* sticker that he held up in a plastic baggie for the jury to see."

Next up was Christine's best friend and my cousin, Zona.

We walked back to my office, and the first task was to make sure Debbie Baker was ready to go. Sandy was going to make sure by picking her up in the morning. Zona would not be a long witness. So, we had two witnesses to go, and no indication that the defense had any witnesses. We were almost certain the defendant would not take the stand.

The following morning was another hot day. It was Thursday, and after we rested our case, we would have the weekend to prepare for the defense and closing argument.

We met Zona at the courthouse, and she was ready and prepared. As I told all witnesses, just tell the truth, don't answer if you don't understand the question, and only answer what you are asked.

Zona took the stand that morning, and she was amazing.

"Zona, can you tell us how you know Christine Stone and your relationship with her?" I asked.

"Christine was my best friend. She was everything I wasn't."

"What do you mean?"

"She was so smart and super athletic, and everyone loved her.

She was so positive, even when others would make fun of her big curly hair… like you did, Anthony," Zona said with a smile.

"We met in grade school, and she would come over to my house at least once a week. We would listen to music. We wore out The Monkees album and literally wore out The Archies 45, "Sugar, Sugar," dancing and singing to that song every time we played it. She always said music motivated her, and she loved the whole era, including the television shows like *Batman* and *Voyage to the Bottom of the Sea.* But she really loved the Monkeys and the *flower power* trend. She had a crush on Davey Jones, but who didn't?"

"Tell me about the *flower power* trend?"

"Well, back then, flower stickers were the cool thing, as well as patches you could sew on your jeans."

"Did Christine have those stickers or patches?"

"I'm not sure about the patches, but she had plenty of stickers. Of course, the first ones she had were given to her by you. She loved them."

I waited for an objection, but none came. Even Vance knew better than to attack a victim and her life.

"Zona, when was the last time you saw Christine?"

"She had come to my house. I believe, the summer after the 6th grade."

Zona began to choke up, and tears flowed down her cheeks.

"Zona, do you need a break?"

"No, it's okay. I just miss her so much. She would have been so good for this world, a true leader," Zona replied. "She came over upset as her father wanted to move them back to Oklahoma, and she didn't want to go. We took a ride to Circle K, and we had a long talk. I told her she should stay with her family and that we would always be friends."

"Why did you tell her that? She wanted to run away and was told to leave all her friends. That was the last time I saw her. However, after that, she left me a note at home. She was upset as I believe the Baker boys had taken her bike."

"OBJECTION!" Vance exclaimed.

"Sustained, disregard the last statement as it's hearsay," Judge Warren said.

"Have you seen or heard from her since then?" I asked.

"I'm sorry to say... no."

"I have no further questions, Your Honor."

"Cross-examination?"

"Yes, Your Honor," Vance stood up and came forward.

"Ms. Montes, isn't it true you received a *flower power* sticker in your mailbox recently?"

"Yes, with no address or return address, just a sticker."

"Could it possibly be from Christine?"

"OBJECTION, Your Honor! This is outrageous!" I shouted.

"She can answer," Judge Warren said. "Ms. Montes."

"No, she would have left me a note."

"No further questions."

"Mr. Garcia?" Judge Warren looked at me.

"Yes, please," I said. "Zona, where do you believe this *flower power* sticker came from?"

"It was a threat, as far as I'm concerned, not to testify. A subtle message from him," Zona replied as she pointed at Clyde and his buddy Peter.

"OBJECTION, Your Honor!"

"Well, you opened the door, Mr. Wright." Judge Warren said. "Mr. Garcia?"

151

"As we heard in one of the wiretap calls, Clyde asked Mr. Ramirez to threaten witnesses and my own family. You will hear testimony from our next witness that will make this relevant."

"Okay, counsel, the answer will be allowed at this time. Anything further at this time?"

"No, Your Honor."

"Well, let's take our lunch break at this time. I will see you all back in court at 1:30 PM. Jurors, as indicated before, please do not discuss this case with anyone outside this courtroom," Judge Warren instructed.

Trial lunches were in my office and consisted of a peanut butter and jelly sandwich. We were also going to talk with Debbie Baker prior to taking the stand this afternoon. Sandy had picked her up, and they continued to have a good relationship. That is one of trust between a detective and a key witness.

"Debbie, how are you?"

"I'm scared, but I'm ready to tell the truth. My dad is evil, and he continues to try and control me with threats. I want to live my life free of him with my kids."

I told Debbie I understood and all we want is the truth and justice for Christine as I looked at her photo on my office corkboard.

We finished up, and I headed to court with Liter as Sandy escorted Debbie to the courtroom. The courtroom was packed with the defendant's *club members* in an attempt to intimidate as well as the press and the general public.

Debbie took the stand, and as she raised her shaking right hand, I saw her look directly into her father's eyes. As I looked over, he turned his head, and Mr. Tough Guy couldn't even look at his daughter. That told me a lot.

"Ms. Baker, may I call you Debbie?"

"Yes, sir. How do you know the defendant, Clyde Baker?"

"He's my dad."

"When was the last time you spoke with your dad?"

"It was a few weeks ago on the phone. He called me collect from prison."

"What was the conversation about?"

"Well, I thought he was calling to see how the kids and I were doing, but that's not why he called at all."

"What do you mean?"

"He first called to tell me detectives came to see him about that missing girl from thirty years ago. He told me if they come to see me, don't say a word."

"Did you ask him why?"

"I asked him if he had something to do with the missing girl."

"What did he say?"

"He got angry and said, 'Hell, no. I don't kill girls, although she was a pain in the ass, and she thought she was all that,' and that he couldn't stand her and all her friends."

"Was that the last time you spoke with him?"

"No, he called after Detective Sandy, and that detective next to you came to see me. I told him the detectives came to see me, and I told them about the old stingray bike you fixed up for me, you know, the purple one. He got really angry and told me to keep my mouth shut."

"Can you describe the bike?"

"Yes, it was a purple Schwinn stingray with a cool banana seat and a flower sticker below the handlebars."

"Do you still have it?"

"No, it was years ago when I was a kid, and it has since been lost during several moves in my life."

"Have you been threatened before your testimony today?"

"OBJECTION!"

"Overruled, you may answer."

"Yes, as I said, my dad and his friend, Peter, who came by and told me not to talk to you or the detectives."

"Okay, thank you. I have nothing further, Your Honor."

"Cross-examination, Mr. Wright?"

"Yes, Your Honor," Vance said. "May I call you Debbie?"

"Sure."

"You indicated your dad gave you a bike when you were younger. Is that correct?"

"Yes, it was pretty cool."

"And where is that bike today?"

"In the dump, for all I know. It finally rusted out and fell apart. It was old, you know."

"So, your father was a good dad?"

"Well, yes and no. He was good to me but not so good to my mother."

"What do you mean?"

"She's dead because of him, and he was mean to her."

"OBJECTION!" I raised my voice.

"You asked, overruled," Judge Warren said.

"You mean she was caught in the crossfire in some gang dispute."

"Yes, that's how she died."

"But your father didn't actually kill her?"

"No."

"Have you ever seen or met your Uncle Jessie?"

"I have not."

"And, of course, you weren't aware of any of the circumstances surrounding the missing person, Christine Stone?"

"I wasn't born yet, no."

"I have nothing further, Your Honor."

"Re-direct Mr. Garcia?" Judge Warren asked.

"Yes," I said. "Are you afraid of your dad?"

"OBJECTION!"

"Overruled, you may answer."

"Yes!"

"Nothing further, Your Honor."

As we walked Debbie out of court, she was literally shaking. We thanked her for her testimony. She turned to Sandy and said, "Do you think he really killed her?"

We all responded *yes!* We also said he might have been helped by her uncle, but we may never know that.

It was time to prepare for the closing argument. We seriously doubted that the defendant would take the stand, but we would prepare for that as well, just in case.

Chapter 23

Closing Argument

As we anticipated, the defendant, Clyde Baker, would not take the stand. In fact, the defense felt like they didn't need to put on any witnesses as they would rely on the standard of proof beyond a reasonable doubt. They would also argue that this was a *no-body* case.

I spent all weekend preparing and not sleeping well, with several late-night conversations on the phone with Liter. We both agreed we had the right man, and the circumstantial evidence was overwhelming. At least we told ourselves that.

I chose a dark blue suit, white shirt, and blue tie. You have to be comfortable when asking a jury to return a guilty verdict. However, more important than that, you had to have credibility with the jury.

The morning was extra warm on this 5th day of August; yes, it was my birthday, but that celebration would have to wait. My kids were very excited to give me my gift, but we agreed to wait until after today's proceedings.

We entered the courtroom, and it was packed again. Mrs. Stone and her sons, Christine's brothers, had a seat in front, thanks to Sandy. I approached them before Judge Warren took the bench. I told them we pray justice will be served, but no matter what happens, I am sorry about the loss of Christine. Mrs. Stone thanked Dean and me for our work.

As we took out seats at the counsel table, Judge Warren took the bench. And before she brought the jury in, she called us up to the front of the bench, including Liter. She had made a ruling in our favor denying what is called a 118 motion. The defense had argued we hadn't proved our case, and they wanted a dismissal. As we approached the bench, she said, "Mr. Garcia, I will let the jury decide this case, but it sure is not the strongest case I have presided over." She then looked at Detective Liter and said, "good luck. You're going to need it. Are we ready to proceed?"

"Yes, Your Honor."

"Oh, and one more thing, Mr. Garcia. The jurors put a small fund together as they noticed the hole in the soles of your shoes when you were sitting at the counsel table."

"What?" I looked down, and sure enough, there was a hole. "Thank God for good socks. I will thank them after the trial," I said as Liter shook his head with his typical smirk, the same one he made when I didn't follow through on my golf shots.

We sat down, and Liter said, "Well, Tony, that was nice of

the judge to tell us that our case sucked."

"No kidding!"

The jurors were brought in, and it was *showtime*. Yes, I was a Laker fan, and that's how it felt before presenting my case. After the judge read them the jury instructions, it was time for me to wake them up.

"Mr. Garcia, are you ready to proceed?"

"Yes, Your Honor."

"Ladies and gentlemen of the jury, thank you for your service, and, at this time, I would like to summarize the case you have heard.

"This is a circumstantial evidence case, and as the judge read in a jury instruction, there are two types of evidence, namely direct evidence and circumstantial evidence. The final statement draws no distinction between them, and either can prove a case beyond a reasonable doubt. How to distinguish direct evidence is as follows: let's say you catch your child eating a cupcake before dinner. He had it in his hand, and you saw him take a bite. That's direct evidence. Suppose, on the other hand, you didn't actually see him take a bite, but you saw a cupcake missing. You found your son in his room with frosting on his face and a cupcake wrapper on the floor in his room. Did he eat the cupcake? Of course, he did. That is circumstantial evidence. Let's talk about this case.

"Christine Stone was a smart, energetic loved young girl that had her whole life ahead of her. She was also a tough girl, and until her last day, she stood up to bullies, as I pointed at the defendant. I'm sure the defense will argue that this is a *no-body* case. But, as testified by Forensic Anthropologist Anderson, he determined that it was an adolescent female by the smoothness of the bones and the other facts he gathered from Detective Liter. Detective Liter collected the victim's shoes, P.F. Flyers, which were pretty much deteriorated, but still had their label attached. And, of course, the flower sticker in the pocket of the jeans. We know for a fact that Christine loved these stickers, and we truly believe it was her remains that were discovered some thirty years later."

I looked over at Mrs. Stone, and she had her head down as she had always hoped Christine had just run away… forever.

"Now, let's take a look at the evidence that ties the defendant to the murder of Christine. Depending on your age, how many remember this bicycle?"

I showed a picture of a Schwinn Stingray dated 1968 from an ad in a Sears catalog.

"These were the best things ever, a banana seat, sissy bar, and slick back tire. We all loved them and rode for miles on them. Well, Christine had the bike and, by all indications, loved it. She put her own mark on her bike, the *flower power* sticker.

"The evidence shows that the defendant and his brother assaulted Christine and stole her *stingray*. This was corroborated later as the defendant gave that same bike to his daughter, Debbie. As his daughter testified, the defendant got angry with her as she told Detective Smith about the bike her dad gave her. Does that fact alone prove he committed the murder? No, but it's a huge part of the puzzle. You heard the testimony of her best friend, Zona, and all the facts she shared regarding the last days she saw Christine.

"Then our Sheriff's Homicide team did an excellent job setting up *wires* on the defendant's phone as well as that of Peter Ramirez. You have the transcripts of those wire conversations in evidence, and as jurors, you can listen and read them during your deliberations. But I would direct you to the following on the call between the defendant and Peter Ramirez."

I then played the following for the jury members:

Peter: *"What the hell did happen? I'm trying to clean up, and this doesn't help."*

Clyde: *"Look, my brother and I tackled her, and we went back to take care of business and you don't want to know about that."*

Peter: *"Did you do her in?"*

Clyde: *"Well, let's just say my brother was the last to see her, but I may have helped a little. As I said before, she had it coming."*

"Had what coming? Murder? A key is they went back to *take care of business*. Again, you have the tapes and transcripts from those conversations and those with his daughter, Debbie.

"Finally, why the threats to Debbie, a direct threat not to testify or else...? Or the flower sticker in Zona's mailbox, as circumstantial threat to keep her mouth shut. Why? Because he is guilty!

"Ladies and gentlemen of the jury, it wasn't a long trial, but we truly believe we presented the evidence to prove the defendant committed the murder of Christine Stone. Some people call these cases cold because of the age of the case, but it's never cold to a family or mother of the victim," I said as I turned to look at Mrs. Stone.

"We have proven this case beyond a reasonable doubt, and we believe you should find the defendant guilty of the murder of Christine Stone. Thank you."

"Defense, ready?"

"Yes, Your Honor."

"Proceed, Mr. Wright."

"Ladies and gentlemen, as you can see, we presented no evidence as the burden is on the prosecution to prove their case beyond a reasonable doubt, which they did not. Also, circumstantial evidence can have two interpretations: one reasonable and the other unreasonable. We believe all the facts presented are unreasonable to prove someone guilty of murder.

"First, we are not even sure the skeletal remains found in the field were even Christine Stones. Forensic Anthropologist Anderson had to admit on cross-examination that he could not say for sure that the remains were Christine's. So, do we have a victim? Ladies and gentlemen, she could walk through that door as he pointed to the courtroom doors. Remember, she wanted to run away, according to the testimony of her best friend, and she was not happy at home. But let's say you believe it's her. What evidence do we have on my client? Chatter on the phone with his good friend, Peter, and his daughter? He never once said he killed

164

anyone! Yes, I'll admit he had Christine's bicycle, but that doesn't equal murder. Kids will be kids. Yes, that's what they were that summer.

"Now, my client may not have the best record and, as you heard, is in prison on other matters, but not for violence. As far as being a member of a local motorcycle gang, that has zero to do with this case.

"As you sit there and look at my client, you may not like him, but your verdict has to be based on facts, not personal feelings.

"Finally, where is his brother? Out at sea? We will never know his involvement."

"OBJECTION, Your Honor... third-party culpability. You can't blame another without proof."

"Objection sustained. Jurors disregard that statement," Judge Warren said. "Move on, Mr. Wright."

"Well, it doesn't matter as there is no reasonable proof that one: the remains are Christine's, and two: there is no evidence that my client committed murder. We ask you to return a verdict of not guilty! Thank you for your service."

"Rebuttal argument, Mr. Garcia?" Judge Warren asked.

"Yes, just briefly."

"Ladies and gentlemen, the defense wants it both ways. First, he argues that the remains found were not Christine's. Of course, they were. Smooth bones, the right age, clothing, and the flower sticker found in her jeans were her trademark. A beautiful girl whose life was taken way too early.

"Second, he wants you to believe if you think it's her, there was not enough evidence to convict the defendant. I won't go over all the facts again, but if you consider the totality of all the facts, this defendant is guilty of the murder of Christine Stone. Thank you. I have nothing further, Your Honor."

As I sat down at the counsel table, I was exhausted. It was a relief to finally give the case to the jury. The jury read final instructions, and before they were sent into the jury room to deliberate, one juror, Mrs. Ramos, pointed to my shoe, smiled, and shook her head. At least I believe I had credibility with them, and they felt sorry for me. Maybe?

"You need to stop walking like you're on skates," Liter said.

"Very funny, Dean."

We hugged Mrs. Stone, and I headed back to my office. We told her as soon as we heard anything, we would call her. The Homicide Team went off to solve another murder.

This was the toughest time for a trial lawyer as you waited for a verdict. It felt like that ride in my dad's car with two popsicles in my pocket, not knowing how it was going to end. It was best to stay busy and to hurry and wait… whatever that meant.

I sat in my chair and looked up at Christine's picture. I said a prayer and told her I did everything I could to seek justice for her. It was time to go home to my family, oh and my birthday cake.

Chapter 24

I was in the 5th grade when I was selected to be the school's projectionist. Why me? It was a huge job. I had to roll out the projector on its stand with wheels. It was two big reels with the film reel loaded on the back, and you had to thread the film tape through various small sprockets until it reached the front wheel. Once threaded, you had to make sure there was some slack so as not to stop the film or even burn it while playing. And I thought square dancing was scary!

Well, the first film I was scheduled to show was for the entire school in the auditorium/lunchroom. It was a 1956 short film called *The Red Balloon*. A fantasy comedy-drama filmed in Paris, France. I was hoping I wouldn't screw this up as it was only thirty-five minutes long. I loaded the film first thing in the morning, and the best thing was it got me out of Math class. The projector had its own light, and as I did a trial run, it kept skipping. I was a nervous wreck. As I sat there, I saw Christine putting up the American flag on the school's flagpole. That was her job. I stepped outside and said good morning.

"Good morning, Anthony. What's the matter, you look down?"

Christine knew me so well.

"I'm showing my first film to the entire school, and I'm a nervous wreck."

"You will be great, I'm sure of it. I look forward to watching the movie. If it helps, I'll sit next to you."

"That would be great, Christine. I may need some moral support."

The 9 AM bell rang, and all the classes lined up to see the movie. Waiting for the 9:30 start time was like waiting for the doctor to put that damn wood tongue depressor in my mouth. My brother always choked and cried, but I didn't. That's not to say that I liked it.

The classes came in loud and hyper, but before the film started, they knew it was quiet time. As I loaded the film, the lights were shut down, and the film worked! I looked at Christine, and she smiled while holding her arms out with her palms up.

The movie was amazing. It was about a young boy in Paris who becomes friends with a red balloon that follows him all over the town and to school. It was a beautiful relationship, but the underlying theme was good vs. evil. A group of young bullies chase the red balloon and finally corner it, throwing rocks and slingshots at it. The balloon gets hit, and it deflates and dies. His best friend is distraught and kneels by the deflated balloon. Then an amazing thing happens. Balloons from all over the world come out of windows and the sky. Red, blue, green, yellow, all the colors you could think of. They come down to the young boy, and as he grabs their strings, they lift him up to the heavens.

I had tears in my eyes, and as I looked over at Christine, she had tears running down her cheeks with a smile on her face. The entire auditorium cheered and clapped, and it was a magical moment for me. Needless to say, Christine was my red balloon, and I'm not sure what that meant, but it felt warm and good. That year was so fun, and I wished it would never end.

Chapter 25

It had been four days, and the jurors were still out. They had a couple of questions regarding the law but nothing else. As I sat in my office, I tried to work on other cases, but it was difficult. The wait was like the time I had projector duty in elementary school. It was stressful, to say the least. As I reflected on those times, I remembered the film *The Red Balloon* and how it is still one of my favorite movies that I enjoy watching with my children. As I thought of Christine, I saw her as that balloon and the Baker brothers as the evil characters. I truly believe that movie made me choose the profession of a prosecutor. I have a passion for victims of crimes, and it drives me every day. As I sat there, the phone rang. Verdict? No such luck. It was Liter checking in.

"Tony? Just checking in."

"Nothing yet, Dean, but you'll be the first call I make."

"Well, we have another *cold case.* A murder from 1984. Let's talk soon as I really think we should start a cold case homicide unit in partnership with our office, and you would be the perfect partner."

"That sounds great, Dean, but I'm not sure DA Mathews would go for it. The word I hear is that he is retiring and won't run again."

"You really should think about putting your name in the hat for District Attorney."

"Well, that's a lot of work, and I love trying cases. But right now, all I can think about is this jury. I hope they haven't seen the classic movie *Twelve Angry Men*."

"Well, hang in there, Tony. You did one hell of a job."

It was now day eight—the longest a jury had ever been out. My thoughts were that we would have a hung jury. The law said we had to have a unanimous decision, and I'm not sure that was going to happen. The other scenario was an acquittal, and I tried not to think about that.

I did my daily lunch workout at the gym, 24-Hour Fitness, as it kept me physically fit, but, more importantly, it was a great stress reduction. It was great for my mental well-being.

As I got back to my office to eat my peanut butter and jelly sandwich, my phone rang. It was the bailiff from Judge Warren's courtroom. Tony, we have a verdict, and the judge wants to read it as soon as possible, as the jury has been here a long time. I asked for an hour to have time to contact family and my team, and it was granted.

I called Dean and the Homicide Team. Sandy would pick up Mrs. Stone. Christine's brothers had left back for Oklahoma as they had to get back to work. The word had spread through the office. It was buzzing with anticipation. As for myself, I was anxious but calm. I had gone to 7:30 Mass that morning at Sacred Heart Church. Having been raised Catholic, it was a good way to start the day and to keep me calm.

Liter met me in the office, and we walked over. The courtroom was packed, and Mrs. Stone was sitting in the front row with Sandy. There were attorneys from both offices in the room, including District Attorney Greg Mathews. That was a first for me.

We greeted several folks in the courtroom as a reporter asked me, "How are you feeling, Anthony?"

"I'm good, thank you."

Really? I feel like the world is on my shoulder. Justice can be very heavy, but I wasn't going to tell him that.

Liter and I took our seats at the counsel table, where Public Defender Wright and Clyde Baker were already seated. Clyde looked over at me with a smirk on his face. Some things just don't change.

The jurors were brought in, and you could hear a pin drop. Several jurors looked at Clyde and at me, as well. It was tough to read them, so I stopped trying years ago.

Judge Warren took the bench. "I understand you have a verdict?"

The jury foreperson, Mrs. Ramos, stood up and said, "Yes, Your Honor."

"Bailiff, please take the verdict forms and hand them to my clerk."

The Court clerk read them and then handed them to the judge. I swear it was all going in slow motion.

"All Rise."

As we all stood, I could hear Mrs. Stone crying in the background, and as I looked back at her, I prayed she would be okay no matter what the verdict was.

Judge Warren then read the results. "We, the jury, find the defendant GUILTY, verdict 1A of First-Degree Murder."

The entire courtroom stood and cheered, and my emotions almost overcame me. Judge Warren asked for order in the court.

174

She then polled the jury, which always made me nervous. One by one, she would ask, "Is this your true verdict?" All said *yes.*

The defendant threw his file at his attorney, and he was escorted back into custody. Sentencing dates were set, and the jurors were thanked and released. The judge told them the admonition not to discuss this case with anyone was now lifted, and she thanked them for their service. I turned and hugged Mrs. Stone. She thanked us all but would give all this up to have her beautiful daughter back. We understood, and I wished the same.

In the hallway, several jurors were waiting to talk with me. They said it was a tough decision, but all the evidence pointed at the defendant. They went over the evidence multiple times. Several jurors started out saying not guilty, but they changed their minds when they looked again at the totality of the evidence. They then handed me an envelope and said here's some money for some new shoes. I thanked them but told them that it would not be appropriate and to please spend it on themselves. We talked about Christine, and they all said she sounded like a wonderful young girl. I left them to talk with the press.

District Attorney Mathews shook my hand and said, "Come see me tomorrow morning. I want to talk about your future." As he left, I turned to Dean and gave him a *man hug,* you know, sideways.

"HA! Everyone, including the judge, didn't give us a chance of succeeding. They have no idea what a team we have!"

"You're damn right, Tony. Now let's go across the street for a celebratory cheer as the team and others are waiting for us at *Court Street West,* the local bar for all involved in the justice system, including judges."

"Sounds good!"

When I got back to the office, I called Rachel and told her the great news. She congratulated me and said she always believed in me. I told her I would be late as I was joining the team at Court Street. She said, "Enjoy. You deserve it."

I looked up at Christine's picture and said, "We did it. I threw that hail Mary pass to you as we did in grade school, and like always, you caught it." I touched her face and headed across the street.

Chapter 26

The bar was alive. It was Thursday, but there was no trial on Fridays, so the trial lawyers usually had a drink on this day.

As I walked in, I saw the group of Superior Court judges in their normal booth, but I decided to stay away as Judge Warren was with them, and we still had sentencing to do on my case. The team was at the bar, and as I headed toward them, they all stood and high-fived me. At the end of the day, these cases always felt like a sporting event with coaches and players on both sides.

To my surprise, my dad was there as he would hang out every now and then with the older attorneys, those that started drinking at noon. He gave me a big hug and called me *boy* as he always did and said the first drink was on him. The Sheriff's Department had done a great job of patrolling his house, and he hadn't had a problem since. We had a drink together, and then he headed home.

I couldn't buy a drink for the rest of the night. The team and I discussed the case and their newest cold case investigation. The conversation then changed to me running for District Attorney. They truly believed the Sheriff's Association would be behind me, along with all of the law enforcement in the county. I said that's a big step but that I would talk to my wife about it soon.

The night wore on, and folks started heading out the door. The last to leave was Liter.

"Tony, it's always great to work with you. I hope we do it again, at a different level, in the near future. Do you need a ride home?"

"No, I'll be okay. I switched to water a few Jack and Cokes ago."

"Okay, I'll give you a call next week."

I sat there drinking my water, thinking about the day and taking the day off tomorrow to hang out with the kids. Then it would be back to work on Monday. Fighter pilots don't stay down long.

The bartender, Jean, who I had known for several years now, got my attention as I was staring off into space.

"Tony."

"Yes?"

"It looks like there is someone here to see you."

As I turned around on the bar stool, there stood a woman with hair like Diana Ross to her shoulders and big round beautiful eyes.

"Anthony, I hear you've been looking for me?"

My heart literally stopped. Christine?

Epilogue

Clyde and Jessie were chasing me down the street, but I knew I was faster than them, except for the fact that Clyde had my stingray. I headed towards the silos, my favorite hiding place. However, as I reached them, Clyde jumped off my bike and pushed me down. I started to fight back, but Jessie finally caught up and held me down as they started to laugh and take my shoes off.

"We always wanted a pair of these," Jessie said with a laugh.

Right then, I heard the sound of a loud pick-up truck, and I knew it could only be one person. I screamed for my dad, and Clyde jumped on my bike and rode off, but before Jessie could get away, my dad threw him against the silo, and it looked like he was out cold. He told me to go to the truck now! I stayed there for several minutes, and as he came back, he asked me if I had any of those flower stickers.

I pulled my last one out and asked, "Why, Dad?"

He grabbed his shovel out of the back of his truck and went back to the silo. When he came back to the truck, he was full of sweat and dirt. He got into the cab and said, "It's a good thing the silos are being filled with grain tomorrow." He told me never to mention this to anyone.

Dad then drove me to the Greyhound Station. I want you to go to Aunt June's in Oklahoma. We will be there in two weeks. Do not say a word about this to anyone! Well, I got on the bus, and I was confused but happy to get out of town at this point. I didn't stop in Oklahoma. My father gave me too much money, so I kept going to New York City, where I knew I had an older cousin, Tim. He had always told me I was welcome to come out whenever I was ready. Well, I was ready now.

In New York, I grew up fast. I changed my name to Michelle after the Beatles song and was emancipated. That's a long story. While there, I met the love of my life, Francisco, who was teaching Art in my Art class. He was from Florence, Italy. We fell in love and moved to Florence and opened a small café there. It's a beautiful country, and I had my own Art studio where my oil paintings were now sold in front of our espresso machine. It was several years since I saw my family, but I decided to move forward, not back. Late in life, we had a son. I named him Antonio, Anthony, of course, as he was someone I did miss. Over time, I thought perhaps we would reconnect.

Five years later, I opened the Sunday New York Times in our café. A treat I gave myself. I couldn't believe my eyes. There was a picture of Anthony at an international prosecutor's conference. They were talking to him about the American Justice System and what they call a *cold case,* and there it was, my name, Christine Stone, killed in 1970. It took my breath away. I went home and told Francisco I had to go to America. He understood. I also wanted to take my son.

As always, Antonio was flying around the football field— soccer in our world. He was so fast... I knew where that came from. I called him over and said, "Anthony," I called him that at times, "we are going to America to finally meet your *nonna* (grandma in Italian)."

He said, "Okay, Mamma, but can I take a picture of that balloon you painted for me? It's my best friend."

"Of course, you can."

Made in the USA
Las Vegas, NV
16 April 2023

70662209R00105